Blaster disaster

Now, I want you to really see the next moment. There's me, just about to lie back down on the couch, thinking hard about how I'm going to explain to Mrs. Matthews why I haven't got any shorts on for the first day of school. And on the radio Yabba Davies is shutting up this thoughtful man by saying, "Let's see what other people think."

Well—it wasn't other people who came on the air. The voice that suddenly tore out of the blaster was my mom's! I was so terrified I clung to the couch. It took me a few seconds to understand what was happening. My mom, Suzy Jollifer, was screaming furiously out of our radio.

Other Bullseye Books you will enjoy

Erin McEwan, Your Days Are Numbered by Alan Ritchie
Germy Blew It—Again! by Rebecca C. Jones
The Lives of Christopher Chant by Diana Wynne Jones
The Sisters Impossible by James David Landis
Witch Week by Diana Wynne Jones

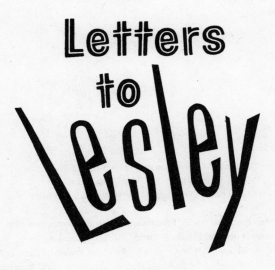

Letters to Lesley

JANICE MARRIOTT

BULLSEYE BOOKS • ALFRED A. KNOPF
NEW YORK

For Robert, and Brian

A BULLSEYE BOOK PUBLISHED BY ALFRED A. KNOPF, INC.
Copyright © 1989 by Janice Marriott
Cover art copyright © 1991 by Mark Buehner

Library of Congress Cataloging-in-Publication Data
Marriott, Janice.
Letters to Lesley / Janice Marriott.
p. cm.
Summary: Twelve-year-old Henry plots to solve all of his life's
problems by marrying his eccentric mother off to his new pen pal's
wealthy, successful father.
ISBN 0-679-81595-3 (pbk.) — ISBN 0-679-91595-8 (lib. bdg.)
[1. Mothers and sons—Fiction. 2. Pen pals—Fiction. 3. New
Zealand—Fiction.] I. Title.
PZ7.M3485Le 1991
[Fic]—dc20   90-41406

RL: 6.0
First Bullseye edition: August 1991

Manufactured in the United States of America
10 9 8 7 6 5 4 3 2 1

How it all started

It's the evening of my first day back at school. Mrs. Matthews, our teacher, has told us we've got to write a very detailed account of how we spent our vacation. I like writing and my mom's got a broken leg and it's kind of quiet around here, so I think I'll spend the long evenings ahead writing a true account of my weird May vacation. I once read in the *Woman's Weekly* that writing is a recommended way of sorting out problems. It doesn't matter if I mention people at school. Mom tells me the truth never hurt anyone, and I'll be leaving to go to junior high school next year. But I don't think Mom would be so hot on her "the truth never hurt anyone" phrase if she knew I was writing this story. It's mainly about her, you see.

Well, I guess it all started with my New Year's Resolutions . . .

1

Life's amazing. You can be doing something as ordinary as trying on shorts one minute, and the next minute an event can occur that changes your life. It was the end of January. We'd come back from a pretty choice summer vacation at my gran's place near the beach at Gisborne. I was in my tiny bedroom getting all my school gear together for the new year at school. I tried my school shorts on and discovered they'd shrunk over the summer.

"Mom!" I yelled through the wall. "I need new school shorts!"

Mom was in the living room, teaching herself to knit and listening to Yabba Davies, the talk-show host, on the radio. "I can't hear you," she yelled back.

I took the shorts through to her. "They're too small!"

"Oh, drat!" she said. "I can't afford new ones." And she went back to her knitting and listening to the call-in show. It's moments like this she seems a very unsatisfactory mother. I mean, whoever heard of a twelve-year-old boy going to school with no shorts on?

"But, Mom—"

"Shut up! I'm listening!"

I sat down on the couch and listened too. This guy was telling Yabba that he thought single parents couldn't possibly bring their kids up properly. If they worked they were too busy to look after them, and if they didn't work they didn't have enough money.

"Yeah, yeah," said Yabba. "What yer gonna do about it, man?"

1

And the guy, who had a soft, slow voice and sounded quite reasonable to me, said something about how single parents shouldn't be allowed to bring up their children alone: something about there being enough males and females around for everyone to be in pairs, and—

Well, I never did get to hear any more of this because Mom transformed herself into a raging maniac and leaped up, scattering balls of wool, needles, and Supercushion, our cat, in all directions. One ball of wool landed in her cup of coffee, which was on the carpet by her chair. She didn't even stop to blame me for it. She rushed straight into the kitchen to the telephone and started dialing.

I thought she was phoning her friend Jill. She might have forgotten to tell Jill something important about work. I took the cup and the sodden wool into the kitchen and came back into the living room to calm Supercushion, who was racing around the room and up the curtains with a tangled mess of wool around his middle.

Now, I want you to really see the next moment. There's me, just about to lie back down on the couch, thinking hard about how I'm going to explain to Mrs. Matthews why I haven't got any shorts on for the first day of school. There's Supercushion, upside down under Mom's chair, with manic eyes staring crazily, fighting a thousand yellow wool snakes. And on the radio Yabba Davies is shutting up this thoughtful man by saying, "Let's see what other people think."

Well—it wasn't other people who came on the air. The voice that suddenly tore out of the blaster was my mom's! I was so terrified I clung to the couch. It took me a few seconds to understand what was happening. My mom, Suzy Jollifer, was screaming furiously out of our radio, raving about "men like that" and being "sick to death of having other people tell me what's good for me" and "how would he like . . . ." and—oh—I couldn't tell you more. I was in agony.

Her voice would be all over Wellington—maybe all over New Zealand! I shuddered. It was too awful, too hideous even for me to cope with.

I think I blacked out. When I came to, Mom was standing by the blocked-up fireplace with her hands on her hips. I hate her standing like that. I think she's trying to look like Superwoman and it doesn't work. I was shriveled up into a corner of the couch, in obvious need of medical attention.

"Well, did you hear that?" she crowed. "I showed him! I hope you're proud of me. I won't sit still and let some sexist upper-class twit tell the world what I should be doing. Eh, Henry?"

And she fired me a look that I think was meant to make me feel as though she'd done it for me. The look completed the shriveling process. It dehydrated me instantly. I felt like a dried-up pea.

"Well, what d'you think, Henry? Did I give him what for?"

"Mom." Somehow I stood up. I had to look straight at her and force her back to earth so she'd take some notice of me and the really important issues of the moment. "Mom," I pleaded, "it's serious. My school shorts have shrunk."

She looked sort of weird, as though she didn't know what shape to make her face into. Then she sighed, sat down in her chair, and said quietly, "Put your shorts in my workbag. I might remember them tomorrow."

I couldn't bear to watch her untangling all the wool, so I slipped away to my bedroom and closed the door. I was desperate for peace and quiet. I was pretty shattered by what I had just witnessed. My mom on radio showing the whole of Wellington how crazy she's become! Boy, was I in a state!

I couldn't concentrate on emptying my pencil case of all the pencils Gavin Andrews had broken last year, so I opened my Room 6 writing diary. The last thing written in it said:

AMBITION:

*My ambition is to become a rich businessman who controls
the government and the multinationals.*

WHAT I WANT OUT OF MY VACATION:

Peace and quiet.

I sometimes find writing calms me down. I got a pen out
of the pencil case and scribbled it round and round on the
cover of the exercise book. It'd been six weeks since I'd used
it. When the ink started flowing I wrote on the next page:

WHAT I WANT OUT OF THIS YEAR:

*1. Peace and quiet in which to work out my business
schemes.*

2. To get rich.

3.

I stared at 3 for a long time. The trouble was, I couldn't
ever imagine getting peace and quiet in this house. It was the
wrong sort of house and Mom was the wrong sort of mom. I
needed someone quiet and intelligent—like that caller on the
radio—to provide me with a proper office, regular meals, and
stylish clothes, and to introduce me to the right kind of money-
making people who could give me hot tips about investing
my pocket money.

The difficulty was Mom. If she was going to start screaming about single-parent families in public, I didn't have a
chance of attracting the right sort of business partners and I'd
never get a bank loan.

It was a dilemma, but I prided myself on making each
dilemma into a challenge. I'd read about the technique once
in the *Woman's Weekly* over at Joe-across-the-road's.

I sat on my bed and thought. Obviously the first thing was
to stop Mom making broadcasts about single-parent families.
So—what could I do? I looked at the problem this way and

that, and suddenly the answer just came. I would have to stop Mom being a single parent! I'd have to get her married again! Like that nice guy on the radio said, there must be heaps of spare single men around. Then I had a better thought. I wouldn't just get Mom married off to anyone. I understand lots of women marry milkmen. I'd get Mom married off to some rich, quiet businessman. Then she wouldn't have any need to scream and shout on the radio again.

I wrote in the old diary:

3. To get Mom married off.

Then underneath it I wrote, to bring it up to date, THESE ARE MY NEW YEAR'S RESOLUTIONS.

"Henry!"

"Yes?"

"Come and help me, please. I can't untangle all this wool by myself. Just like you to walk away from a problem."

"Coming!"

I walked back into the problem. Supercushion, low to the ground like a Formula One car, with his eyes like headlights, was racing backwards around the couch, dragging yellow snakes of wool. I stopped him with my special tomcat hiss.

"Thanks, Henry. You're a good lad," Mom said as I helped her rewind the wool.

Yes, I thought to myself, I think I must be. I had risen to a challenge and solved a dilemma, and I'd made three New Year's Resolutions. There was no doubt about it—I was a survivor.

As it turned out, thank God I was.

2

The week after the radio incident was terrible. I was struggling with having Mrs. Matthews for a teacher and having to sit next to Rachel Brown. Mrs. Matthews is OK, except that she thinks boys and girls should sit together. Sitting next to Rachel meant I couldn't do any work at all because I couldn't think. Every evening I lay on my bed worried sick that Mom would phone the radio station again. What if it became one of her enthusiasms? I lay there, exhausted with executive stress, talking to Spanzini about NYRs 1, 2, and 3. I was getting nowhere with them.

Just before you think I'm dry-roasted nuts, I'll explain about Spanzini. Spanzini is a furry round creature, the size of a tennis ball, who lives in inner space. He's a collection of vast intelligences and supreme wisdom who recognizes that my problems merit the use of all his powers. I can't feel or see him, of course, because he's in another dimension, but we talk in my mind.

From my reading in the *Woman's Weekly* I've learned that adults often talk to people in their heads. I think they call it fantasizing. Spanzini's much more useful than that. He can feed problems into some computer that hasn't been invented here yet and give me the one true answer. The difficulty was, there wasn't one true answer for the New Year's Resolutions problem. Spanzini said he could only offer suggestions and support.

See, the trouble with all these resolutions is Mom. She's crazy. When Dad lived here, before they became two solo parents, they both used to spend a lot of time watching TV, like normal people. But after she kicked him out, six months ago, she started having enthusiasms. These are crazes for things like gardening, knitting, reading. She calls it "making up for lost time," which shows how mad she is.

I learned to cope with these enthusiasms. The *Woman's Weekly* says women often have bad moods. Something to do with cycling. So I knew I just had to put up with it. But I wasn't prepared for the day her enthusiasms took her away from the privacy of our living room and out into the open air where anyone could see her.

It was like this. I was doing the dishes. Mom was trying to alter my shorts. She didn't look very marriageable, wearing her track suit pants with the stripes gone all wavy, and swearing at the needle.

I started trying to scrape burnt rice out of the saucepan.

"It's unfair," I said.

"Quit moaning," Mom snapped back.

"But you did the easy part, burning the rice. I have to do the hard part, cleaning the bloody saucepan."

"Don't swear."

"Can if I want to."

"You sound like a twit."

An example of Mom's unfairness. She swears all the time. I went on scraping and she went on sewing and swearing. Suddenly she looked up. "Hey! What's holding you up? Leave that pot to soak. Get ready for bed. Jill's coming around to discuss our bike ride for Saturday."

I left the rice pot on the bench. I knew it'd stay there for weeks.

"What bike ride's this, Mom?"

"Oh, I've decided I need to get out a bit, blow the cobwebs away. So Jill and I are going into the Wairarapa on bikes this weekend."

I was staggered. I mean, I was just amazed! A crazy and embarrassing mom can be handled in private by an under-

7

standing child. A crazy and embarrassing mom in public is—well, no child can cope with it, not even me. My mom—kind of lumpy and lazy—on a bike! At least I wouldn't be there to see it. I was going to Dad and Amanda's for the weekend.

"What's wrong with me biking, eh?"

"Nothing. I never said anything."

"No, you didn't have to. Now listen. When Jill comes around I don't want any moans and groans about going to bed."

"OK. Can I watch TV till then?"

"Of course not."

The doorbell rang.

"Oooooo-oooooo! Coming!" shrieked Mom, which was totally unnecessary, as the front door's made of glass, and Jill could see right into the kitchen. We haven't got a hall like ordinary people have.

Jill burst in, shouting, "Suzy, wait till you hear what I've arranged!"

She hugged Mom as though they were meeting at the railway station, when in fact they work together and see each other nearly every day.

"What?" Mom yelled. Jill made her eyes roll up into the back of her head. I wish I could do that but I haven't had the operation.

"You know Ben and Lionel from the bike club? They're definitely coming!"

Jill and Mom then screamed with laughter. I slunk, unnoticed, into my room.

At least it was quieter in there, even though the actual room is the pits. My room is barely large enough for a guinea pig, and it's got a silly babyish bed with a blue-painted headboard and footboard which makes it look as though it's a cemetery for babies instead of a room. There's a table and chair and a built-in cupboard that's supposed to have all my junk inside it every Saturday morning before I'm allowed to phone anyone. The worst thing about the room is the quilt on my bed. It's got teddy bears on it, on both sides of it, and I'm twelve! I've pleaded with Mom for a new one, but she says Nana made it just before she died and I should appreciate it because it's made by hand. I don't. In fact it embarrasses me so much that I never invite friends into my room.

I could hear Mom and Jill through the wall. They weren't watching TV, so a perfectly good electrical appliance was going to waste. They started tittering about whether they'd ride over the Big Hill or get a train to Featherston on the other side. I tried to imagine Mom and Jill on bikes but I couldn't. Mom is large and lumpy, like I said, and this includes her legs. God, I hope she doesn't wear shorts. She wouldn't, would she? Jill is pointed and skinny, with a long ropy neck and a beaky nose. She wears dangly earrings that could so easily get caught in the brake cables of a racing bike. Probably they won't borrow racing bikes. I don't think mothers ride racing bikes.

"Hi, Spanzini. How are you and how is your dimension?"

"Fine, Henry. Enter your problems now."

"Well, Mom's started biking—outdoors."

Our conversations are private, but Spanzini did tell me not to knock Mom's biking enthusiasm because it could lead to the achieving of NYR3. I hadn't thought of that. Suddenly I was very eager to meet Ben and Lionel.

3

The next day, in math, I was hoping to work hard with Spanzini on my NYR problems, but we had a test instead. I thought there might be some time in language but Mrs. Matthews said she had a surprise for us, and just when we thought she was going to tell us she had to go into the hospital, she told us we were all going to get a pen pal in Auckland. Leonard said, "But that's at the other end of the island! It takes all day to drive there!" and Mrs. Matthews explained that we weren't going there, just sending letters. Rachel giggled and said, "What if it's a boy?" and I kicked her, softly, and Mrs. Matthews saw. But Mrs. Matthews didn't realize it was a soft kick, nor did she take into account that Rachel had set up her four smelly heart-shaped erasers on the edge of my desk. So Mrs. Matthews watched me all day, and I had to write my letter to my unknown pen pal as a detention.

Hi! my name is Henry Jollifer and I guess my life is pretty boring and dull except that my mom suffers from enthusiasms. I'll tell you more about these later.

My New Year's Resolutions are:

1. Have peace and quiet.

2. Get rich.

3. Marry my mom off so she's not my responsibility so much.

This might sound strange to you, but in my circumstances, it can be called enterprising. I haven't decided how to achieve these resolutions yet. Any ideas?

What are your favorite TV shows? Do you ride a bike to

school? I do, but people are always letting the air out of the
tires so I have to walk it home. It's boring.

I hope it's going to be fun having a pen pal.
Yours truly,
Henry Jollifer

Then I took my letter to Mrs. Matthews.

"Will that do, Mrs. Matthews?"

She didn't read it. She just checked that I'd done it.

"That's fine. I hope, Henry, that you will treat Rachel and
all girls more sensibly from now on. You will, won't you?"

"OK."

I felt depressed walking home with my flat tire that afternoon. Why couldn't I be biking home to a huge mansion with
a double garage and sliding glass doors, like places on TV
comedies? Why couldn't Mom be arranging flowers or train-
ing a guide dog for the blind? Why didn't she have time to
chat without doing something else at the same time?

I turned the corner and saw our saggy picket fence. It was
an awful moment. What man would want to marry Mom after
he'd seen that fence! Mom was home too. The yellow Mini
was outside. That meant no peace and quiet today.

Supercushion was rolling around on the path. I picked him
up and he purred loudly, then he bit me. I dropped him into
the long grass. Poor Supercushion. He's had a pretty disturbed upbringing. We've had him for six months. Mom got
him to replace Dad.

"Henry, darling! Why are you so late getting home? I've
come home early especially for you. I've got a fantastic idea."

Mom was on our doorstep, waving and shouting at me as
I walked up the path nursing my gouged hand. Everyone in
our suburb could hear her. Thank goodness not absolutely all
of them could see her. She was wearing new pink shorts!

"We should walk up Johnston's Hill and watch the sun go

11

down. It's such a marvelous day. Hurry up, the sun won't wait."

That's my mom. There's an enthusiasm brewing in her. I can tell by the way she asks me thousands of questions and never waits to hear an answer.

"Come on, Henry. Hurry up!"

There was nothing for it. I had to get in the car—in the back seat (what total humiliation)—and go off on a pointless quest to see if the sun would set or not.

"We wrote pen pal letters today," I said as she threw the Mini around a corner and we skidded on the gravel.

"Did you, dear? Oh, look at that sky! Look, Henry! See the ferry! Look! Over there! Just past Soames Island! What a sight! Oh, what a beautiful city! Just look at that blue sea!"

I shut my eyes so I couldn't see the sharp corners coming up. I made a mental note that the guy I got for Mom will have to do all the driving.

Next day I woke up with a cold. I must have caught it up on Johnston's Hill the night before, when the clouds covered the sun so totally that we couldn't tell when sunset actually took place. My ears were sore, too; Mom was slamming kitchen cupboard doors.

"Hurry up! Get up!" she roared.

When I slouched into the kitchen she was writing checks at the table. So I knew she was in her "How are we going to manage?" mood. And that was serious.

I got my cereal and ate it without a murmur. I even made it slide down the back of my throat without any swallowing noise. You just squeeze it around your mouth real slowly till all the lumps kind of dissolve, then you tilt your head back slightly and go all relaxed in your neck. It's taken me six months to perfect it—six months of "How are we going to manage?"

Managing is to do with money. Since Dad left we've only had Mom's earnings to live on. I'm sure that when I grow up I'll be able to manage our household finances much better than Mom does. And I'll make daring investments and get very rich, and Mom will be able to have expensive enthusiasms then, so long as they're quiet ones.

The milk was off slightly, making the cereal taste awful. I didn't dare complain.

"Get me three stamps."

"Yes, Mom."

She banged the stamps on the envelopes she brought home from work, and slapped them into her big bag that always hangs from the back of her kitchen chair in the morning.

"Mom, can I have a stamp, please?"

"Why?"

"I need one for my pen pal letter. We get to go down to the post office to mail them if we've brought a stamp or the money for one."

"Hmmm. I guess so. I wonder how long this interest of yours will last. The trouble with you, Henry, is that you're always starting things and never finishing them."

That is the sort of injustice I put up with silently all the time.

When Mom had revved the Mini up like a Concorde and disappeared down the hill, I went back inside our house, carefully stuck the stamp upside down on the left-hand side of an envelope, and put it in my bag. I chased Supercushion around the kitchen and managed to shoo him out, then I locked the door and went down the path to the shed where I keep my bike.

I rode to school carefully, doing a detour around Box Street because Gavin Andrews lives there. I can't stand him.

I was riding particularly skillfully, one-handed, not riding over a single paint line or crack in the road, when I heard the whir and tiny clicks of a racing bike coming up behind me.

"Commie cretin," Gavin Andrews sneered.

"Blue baboon butt," I replied.

13

Gavin kept level with me. He stood up on his pedals, thwacked his butt with both hands, yelled, "Watch out!" and twisted his front wheel at mine. I braked. He shot ahead and, luckily for me, kept going.

Gavin is one of those big, brutal kids who control the schoolyard. He has a dad who works, a mom who doesn't, an older sister who's real nice, a big clean-looking dog, and a huge new station wagon. He thinks he's as powerful as rocket fuel, so powerful he could crash the sound barrier on his bike.

In language we were allowed to mail our letters. The post office is just around the corner from school. I know it really well because I bank the money there that Dad gives me when I stay with him. I've got an account that pays interest, so I'm waiting for it to grow.

Mary, the woman at the counter, knows me and knows Mom because they used to go to a women's meeting together each week. That was about a year ago. She's the woman who gave Supercushion to Mom. While the other kids were mailing their letters and giggling about what sort of pen pal they'd get, I went in to see Mary. I told her about the pen pals. She said that'd mean she'd be seeing lots more of me from now on. I'd be in and out for stamps, she said.

That disturbed me a bit. I didn't want to have to pay out of my pocket money for my pen pal. I'd have to work out a way of presenting the case to Mom that a pen pal was a necessary part of my education. Then she'd have to pay.

I came out into the sunshine. The others were waiting for me. They watched as my first pen pal letter slid into the slot marked LETTERS—OTHER PLACES.

It's hard for me to believe this now, but at the time I never gave that letter a second thought.

4

That weekend I went to Dad's. It was awful. It's hard to feel I fit in with Dad now that Amanda's got him doing everything differently from how he used to do things. He used to smoke a pipe and I used to fill the bowl for him. Amanda's stopped him smoking. Mom wouldn't let him read the paper at the table. We had to talk to each other. Now he and Amanda eat their meals in silence, reading every paper that's ever been printed.

Both nights I was there, they went out to some political meetings about electoral boundaries and sewage. Not the sort of life you'd think my dad would leave Mom for. He left when Mom discovered he was going out with Amanda. Mom said he should have been spending this time with me. I could see that when Dad wanted to go out somewhere posh to dinner he would prefer to have that dopey woman rather than me sitting across the table from him. He knows I can never see any point in spending a whole evening just having dinner. But Mom couldn't understand this. I didn't mind his not chatting with me at home, or his not helping me with my homework and stuff, because he was always so quiet and sort of worried-looking; he wasn't that great to spend time with. And he was hopeless when he did try to help me with my homework. He doesn't understand numeration and he can't color in borders with felt-tip pens. He says he never had to do these things in his day. What a lie! He manages a garage in town, so he must have had some education.

On Sunday morning Dad took five minutes off from reading papers and clipping articles out of them to talk to me.

"Henry," he said, putting the scissors down quietly, "we must have a chat."

I went bright pink. I'd heard rumors about father-son chats. I'd even read about one in a book Mom had given me. I wasn't having one—not with my own dad.

"You'll be off back to your mom in a few hours and I haven't really talked to you this weekend."

I decided to take the initiative. You really have to with Dad.

"Let's talk about my New Year's Resolutions, Dad."

"Oh. Ah. Yes. I make those too."

"Do you, Dad?"

"Yes. Very seriously. I find that what we often lack in life is a purpose. Life can slip by. I think mine almost did."

He sighed and shifted position and started fiddling with the scissors. I could hear Mom in my head, saying, "Will you look at me, Kev, and stop fiddling when you are talking to me!" But Amanda was in their bedroom writing a speech and it was just Dad and me. I said nothing.

"This year, Henry, I've resolved to work damn hard for the ward. Come election time we're going to get those National ninnies out in this electorate." He suddenly looked quite powerful. I was taken aback. "And you, Henry, what's your resolution this year?"

"Oh, er—" I blushed again. This was worse than the father-son talk. "I, er, I've forgotten," I said, which was real dumb of me.

"Well," said Dad, getting intense about it all, sitting up straight and taking up his pen and a piece of blank paper, "let's write one down."

I stared at the paper for a long time. The trouble with Dad is, he's so serious. It's like religion, or Scout's honor, or that positive reinforcement stuff some teachers do to punish you. Finally I gabbled, "I resolve to help people in distress," and Dad wrote it down. He thought it was for real.

Then he passed the pen to me. I didn't understand at first, then I realized what I was supposed to do. I signed the paper, and he signed it, and he pinned it up on the wall. He looked ever so pleased for some reason.

"There we are, Henry. A resolution you'll keep all year, and a father who's promised to help you."

I felt sort of sad for him then, but I didn't know why. It was one of those feelings that creep up on you. When I looked up from examining the marble pattern on the Formica table-top, Dad was busily cutting out clippings again.

I wandered into the back garden, which was just big enough for the revolving clothesline, and sat on an old concrete house pile. I'm so split between my two parents that I have to have different resolutions in the different houses. I thought about my real resolutions, the NYRs. Right, I thought, I'll apply Dad's seriousness to them and see where it gets me.

I jumped up, hit my head on the clothesline, and rushed inside screaming, "Head injury, make way, make way!"

Amanda came rushing out of the bedroom with a look of horror on her face. "Henry, are you all right?"

" 'Course, sucker. I wouldn't be able to talk if I'd got a head injury!"

I rolled on the floor laughing, and Amanda looked so confused I thought she was going to burst into tears. But she didn't. She went back into their bedroom to keep writing her speech. And she shut the door. You see what I mean by the weekend at Dad's being awful.

5

Mom really did go biking with Jill and a bunch of other people. She twisted her knee and got such a sore backside that she couldn't sit down to read the paper while I was doing the dishes on Monday evening.

"We met the most wonderful people, Henry. I'm sure you'll like them. They're coming for lunch on Saturday. Two really interesting men. They belong to a folk dancing group and they're schoolteachers."

"What!" I let a plate slide back into the water. I needed to retire to my room, lie on the teddy bears, and think about this crisis right away. I needed Spanzini.

I rushed through the saucepans, and before Mom got to the TV pages I was shutting the door of my bedroom and calling up Spanzini.

"Hello, Spanzini. Come in, Spanzini."

"What zup?"

Spanzini always knows when something's urgent. He does away with the official greetings.

"Spanzini, I think Mom is interested in a teacher. Imagine!"

"So? I thought you liked teachers."

"Well, sort of. But not for something to have in the house. And I want a quiet type who never gets cross. Teachers are poor and they're always cross."

"Leave it to me, Henry. I'll see what I can do."

Next Saturday the two folk dancing schoolteachers, Jill, and the postman all arrived at the same time. After all the

18

shouts of "So you *did* get home!" and "How's your back-side?" and "I've got some great photos," Mom glanced down at the mail and yelled, "Henry, a letter!" Then she skipped into the living room with two fat envelopes of photos and two very thin schoolteachers.

We've got a small sunny back garden with one huge wal-nut tree and lots of knee-high grass. Mom's enthusiasm for gardening was last year. She gave up when she discovered that the slugs and snails were more enthusiastic than she was. I lay down in the long grass by the tree. Supercushion had been kicked out of the house. No doubt one of the school-teachers didn't like the way Supercushion refuses to share the couch with anyone. He came and leaned against me, smiling and arching his back. I stroked him and then I took a deep breath and opened the letter.

Dear Henry,
I'm so glad we are pen pals. You sound very interesting. I hope you don't mind if I'm not interesting. I lead a very dull life actually.

First I'll describe my house and family. I have a father. Mom died five years ago. Since then my dad's devoted his whole life to making money. He's always at work, or having weekend conferences on his yacht. He hires a housekeeper to look after me as he hasn't the time. He gives me anything I ask for, but it still seems a boring life.

Our house isn't surrounded by neighbors. It has its own access road and is built into a cliff overlooking Auckland harbor. We have a swimming pool, spa pool, and tennis court, as well as spare bedrooms, so maybe you could come and stay if we write often and become friends.

I must go to violin lessons now. I can hear the taxi tooting.
Write again.
Your pen pal,
Lesley Lacey   *(At school they call me Les.)*

I lay back on the soft grass, the shadow from the walnut tree drifting back and forth over me. I held the letter over my head, between me and the sun. I could see lines running down the paper that I couldn't see when I put the paper on the grass. It was posh paper, like banknote paper. Maybe it was banknote paper.

Supercushion had settled down in a huge black circle beside me. I watched him breathing in and out, up and down. His paws were over his eyes to block out the sun. He looked as happy as I felt. For the first time in my life I was in luck. I had managed to land myself an ideal pen pal. I tried out the name: Lesley Lacey. Not Les. That was too much like my dad's co-workers' names. With Lesley's father's help I would be able to invest my pocket money daringly but wisely, and achieve NYR2.

I made a subsidiary resolution—to reply to each of Lesley's letters promptly. And another resolution—to make a carbon copy of all my letters to Lesley. This pen pal was going to be good enough to warrant a correspondence file, like accountants and lawyers have. Writing to Lesley had what Mrs. Matthews called potential. Maybe I'd get a vacation on a yacht out of it, as a cabin boy. Maybe his father would even pay me for doing cabin boy work! I stretched out, relaxed and undisturbed at last.

At school on Monday I found out that Gavin Andrews's pen pal was a girl, and she wrote in printing instead of joined-up writing. He threw her letter away. Poor old Gavin.

6

Two weeks later Mom's new enthusiasm for folk dancing was driving me mad. She had bought these awful folk dancing records and every evening she danced up and down the living room, panting, "One and a two and a three," or "Slide, slide, stamp, stamp, stamp." I couldn't watch TV and I couldn't even relax with Spanzini. Every time I lay on my teddy bears I found that the whole room was shaking. The squeaky violins screamed into my ears through the wall.

I took to spending the early evenings in the public library, doing heaps of work for school projects. We were doing economics. One day Mrs. Matthews asked me to stay behind. She had her "I hope you realize my concern is only for you" look on, and she'd taken far too much notice of me all day. She got me stacking up math books and she waited until everyone had left, even Rachel, who takes ten minutes to pack her schoolbag. Then she said I looked pale and tired and was I getting enough sleep. I said yes. She said I appeared overanxious about my schoolwork and that I didn't have to do so much homework. I thought this was a bit odd, as she was getting me to work more by making me pile up math books.

I didn't tell her the two problems that were really making me tense—Mom's folk dancing and my not having anything interesting to say in my next letter to Lesley. I just stood there in my drugged gorilla pose.

"I think I'll have to have a talk with your mother," she said. I told her Mom worked.

"Don't we all," she said. I told her Mom was frightened

21

of situations where she might fail, like talking about me. I'd read about this in the *Woman's Weekly*. Mrs. Matthews looked strange, a bit like Supercushion if you offer him the wrong type of sardines, and said was that why I hadn't brought back the notice about parent-teacher interview times. I said yes, and she patted me on the head! Then she made me promise I wouldn't do any homework that evening. I could see her point. The classroom walls were covered with my stories, all made up, about weekends with my uncle on a yacht, or my articles about making money on the stock market.

I biked home with both hands on the handlebars because no one was about and I needed to think hard about my two big problems. Two whole weeks had gone by since I got Lesley's letter, and I didn't have anything to say to him. I needed to meet him. I needed him to introduce me to his influential friends. But I couldn't meet him at home, sitting on the teddy bears. It had to be a more appropriate setting for business conferences. He had to invite me to his place, but how did I go about asking him to?

I rounded the corner of Box Street and pedaled slowly up the home stretch. By now I was onto my second major problem. This was about Mom. I had this New Year's Resolution about marrying her off to someone suitable, but how? This folk dancing schoolteacher was too common a sight at our place. What if he beat me to it? When I got home I might find a note saying, "Got married. On honeymoon. Please feed Supercushion. Love, Mom and Lionel."

I put my bike in the shed and started washing the car. Mom had been picked up by the folk dancing teacher in his Toyota every day that week, so the Mini hadn't been used, but Mom still insisted it was part of my pocket money chores. I was just giving it the final polish when the Toyota returned. Mom and Lionel went inside and very soon I could hear, and so could all the neighbors, the ghastly music they danced to.

I decided to wash the car all over again. When I was polishing the hubcaps and it was getting dark, the music stopped and I could hear a real rip-roaring argument going on. So could all the neighbors. Even the paperboy gave me a sympathetic look when he handed me the *Post*. I went inside.

Both my worries were about to be solved. Spanzini must have been organizing it for me. The solution was so spectacular that when it was all over I sat down and wrote to Lesley about it. I knew he'd understand.

Dear Lesley,
Remember I was telling you how difficult it is with my mom's enthusiasms? Well, here's an example. Just an hour ago her enthusiasm for folk dancing died. It was eliminated, wiped out, terminated, zapped, and a new enthusiasm took its place.

I came up the path after washing Mom's car. I opened the door and—Mom hit me! Right in the nose. She screamed, "Sorry, sorry, darling! I thought you were Lionel." I said it was a funny dance routine, and she said, "No darling. No. I've just chased him out of the house, and when you came in I thought you were him coming back to apologize."

I touched my nose very gingerly and she immediately cuddled me. "Oh, I'm so sorry, Henry."

I managed to shrug her off. "Where'd he go?" I asked. "He didn't pass me on the path."

"That's it then!" yelled Mom. "He's hiding around the back. I knew I couldn't trust him to go."

"But what's happened, Mom?"

"What's happened!" She glared at me as though it was my fault, but I'm used to this.

"That man tried to tell me it was my job to make the dinner and that I should have made it, you know, hand-bloody-made it, for him specially!"

"Ooh, did you make something special?" I asked.

23

She screamed, "No, no, no!" and told me I was growing up to be just like him, then she stormed off.

That made me feel really angry too. How could I grow up to be like a folk dancing schoolteacher? He wore those bells around the bottoms of his trousers when he was dancing. I never wore bells around anything, and I wasn't even related to him.

What would you have done, Lesley? I rushed out the front door and around the back, searching him out. And I found him. He was on the back doorstep putting on his outdoor shoes. He didn't have the bells on. Mom was standing over him calling him "sexist" and "exploiter."

Well, he went after that, and Mom opened a package of Mallowpuffs for us both and I thought we'd have some peace. I was just about to tell her I'd lost my sweater at swimming when Jill came in. "Yoo-hooo, Suzy!" I heard. They chatted and raged on for hours. I went and sat under the walnut tree with Supercushion. (That's my cat. He's very dominant and macho, and we understand each other completely.) We both agreed Mom was a handful.

Mom told me, at dinner, which was very late, that she'd decided to take up hiking! That'll mean more of the pink shorts in public. She gave me the folk dancing records to give to Mrs. Matthews.

I'm worn out. It's so hectic around here. Females are crazy, aren't they? Bye for now. Write soon, like last time.
Harassed Henry

PS Now Mom wants me to go on a hiking vacation with her. She's just brought my cocoa in and told me. Stay tuned for more drama!

I was quite pleased with that letter. I wanted Lesley to know how unsuitable my lifestyle was for someone with a genius for business. I thought it was time I started pushing NYR2. One day Lesley would suddenly realize how his dad could help me, and then, wham, an invite for vacation would be in the next letter.

7

I was hoping for a letter back from Lesley almost immediately but I didn't get one that week. The wait seemed so long that I got tired of sitting around under the walnut tree or lying on my bed talking to Spanzini. I had to do other things to fill in the time.

My major occupation for the next two weeks was choosing the right opportunity to hand the folk dancing records over to Mrs. Matthews. I mean, I couldn't be seen by any other kids when I gave them to her. They'd think I was greasing. There are terrible rumors around our school about what Gavin does to greasers. Of course I'd tried to ditch the dreaded gift at home, but on Tuesday Mom had forced me to take the records to school. As she'd driven me there, I couldn't possibly throw them into a bin on the way. She'd watched me go into the prefab as well. Another life-sized dilemma, another challenge.

I sneaked the records quickly onto the pile of record covers we have in our classroom. It was a brilliant hiding place—a complete camouflage—but they couldn't stay there long, as we were bound to use record covers for art on Thursday. Mrs. Matthews gets them from a record factory.

On Wednesday Mrs. Matthews was furious with me because I'd stuck all Rachel's pink heart-shaped erasers together with jelly from my sandwiches and made a sculpture. Gavin watched me do it at lunchtime. He told on me after Rachel let out a godalmighty wail when she found it. I thought the sculpture was better than most you see around town, although it was on a smaller scale. But Mrs. Matthews saw neither my artistry, nor Rachel's overacting, nor Gavin's telling tales. So there I was, on my own, doing detention again.

I was so busy writing, "I mustn't annoy Rachel" one hundred times that I wasn't watching Mrs. Matthews. I'd just finished the hundredth "mustn't" in a column when a loud crack, like a pistol shot, exploded in my ears. I whipped around, thinking I was being shot at, and there was Mrs. Matthews, the prime suspect, leaping into the air by the guillotine we use for cutting paper. I hurled myself under my desk and watched. She had this look of amazement on her face as she cautiously approached the record covers she'd been slicing. Aha! I realized I wasn't being shot at by Mrs. Matthews. She was slicing record covers, and she'd just sliced through a folk dancing record.

"You've just broken a record, Mrs. Matthews," I said. It was the first thing that came into my head. I didn't mean to be smart. Very slowly, she lifted up the two halves of the record she'd just sliced—a bit like a woman in a shampoo commercial. "It's OK, Mrs. Matthews. I know what they are."

"Oh, you do, do you? Another of your immature little pranks, is it?"

I was worried about her eyes. I really thought they'd pop right out of her tight-skinned face.

"Well, I guess so, Mrs. Matthews." I'd never known folk dancing was immature before. "I brought them to school—for you. They're a gift from my mom."

It was her mouth this time that I focused on. It changed from a thin line to a little hole like in the middle of a record.

"Oh," she said. The sound pulsed out of the hole like a bubble from a bubble pipe. "Oh. Yes. Well. Thank you. Thank your mother very much, Henry. Er, off you go now," she ended in a whisper.

And off I went, leaving a column of "I"'s and a column of "mustn't"'s on a huge piece of computer paper on my desk.

When I got home I checked the mail. There was a Give Generously To Something envelope, a bill from the electricity company, and a long blue envelope, for me, from Lesley! I read it straightaway, under the walnut tree of course.

Dear Henry,
It must be terrible having to listen to fights between your mother and a folk dancing schoolteacher. But it sounds to me as though they do clear the air, the fights I mean.

At home Dad doesn't have fights. He doesn't have mistresses or lovers or girlfriends. He has business associates who come for drinks. These come in either sex. I know they're not really friends because they never sit on the big leather couch by the window. They always sit in armchairs and lean back rather than forward toward Dad. He sighs a lot when he, and I, clean up afterwards. He says everyone is so similar these days, empty-headed, with their mouths full of words. He looks so miserable I often make him a drink so he can recover from the party. I can't see why he goes on having them. Maybe it's some way he has of making money. He's a lawyer and they tend to get rich just by talking.

He doesn't talk much to me when he's in his sad mood. If I ask him what's the matter, he says, "Nothing for you to worry about. You'll be all right," which isn't what I want him to say.

All those people who come for drinks, they don't do anything together. They just drink and talk. I don't think adults have real friends that they do things with.

Perhaps Dad's not really happy because he's not very well. He's got high blood pressure and has to take pills. The doctor's always trying to make him slow down and take vacations but he won't. I wish he would.

Your mom sounds fun. But will she be able to provide you with all the important things when you're older, like exam fees and university tuition? I hope she will. It's unfair that some people don't have as much money as other people.

Well, I've just reread this and it seems such a depressing letter, and yours was such fun to read! So I'll finish it off by telling you a little bit about me and my interests.

I play the violin, as I think I mentioned before, so I have to practice a lot. Every day, when I get home from school, I have to do an hour's practice before dinner, and before Dad gets home. Dad says I'm much too tired after dinner, but I know that really it's because he doesn't like the sound. I have a pet but mine's not like your Supercushion. Mine is a computer, and I use it to do my schoolwork and print out notices, forms, and circulars which I design myself. I like animals but Dad won't let me have one, and the housekeeper's allergic to everything.

And no, I don't bike to school. My school is rather a long way away from here so I go in a taxi. But I can ride a bike and often do ride other people's at school. There's nowhere around the house where I could ride. It's all far too steep.

In answer to another question of yours, I haven't got any favorite TV programs except the news because Dad tells me TV doesn't make use of a growing brain properly and after dinner I either do things for him, for his work, or I go to my room and play on my computer.

I'd better go now as it's nearly bedtime. I'm looking forward to your next letter.
See you,
Lesley

I lay back on the soft unmown grass, my schoolbag under my head. I learned a new word from a TV ad last week: "reverie." Thank goodness I did, because it meant I could now have a reverie and know what I was having. I reveried about Lesley and his computer. I reveried about having people in for drinks who always lean politely back in their chairs. Not like Mom's friends, who either sit on the kitchen table, where I actually eat, or sprawl on the cushions on the floor or, worst of all, lounge on the couch with one leg slung up and over the back of it. I reveried about working hard for Mr. Lacey and achieving NYR2. I passed into a state of altered consciousness and only came back to boring earth and our overgrown garden when I heard Mom yelling, "Henry! Why haven't you put the milk bottles out?"

Mom was home.

8

It was a typical week after that. Mom embarrassed me by signing a Homosexual Human Rights petition when I was shopping with her in Manners Mall. Hundreds of people saw us by the campaign table. Then she went into a natural foods shop that smelled, and she bought all sorts of strange things to make bread with. Everyone else in the shop was very thin, wearing clothes that just hung from their coat hanger shoulders. Mom was the only fat person there. I felt dreadful.

At school Gavin seemed to be seeking me out to be his friend. I decided I'd join his gang now before there was anyone else in it. Then he and I could be the bosses of it. I was making some extra money writing essays for kids in my class, charging fifty cents a one-page story. I'd done two for Gavin, and Mrs. Matthews told him they showed a vast improvement. I even confided in him one wet lunch hour when we were hanging around the bike sheds waiting to catch the creep who lets the air out of tires. I told him about Mom's latest hiking enthusiasm and he laughed. He said his dad took him on hikes and overnight camps to make a man of him. I felt real sympathy for Gavin. I mean, imagine having a dad who didn't know whether his son was male or female. But then I thought again and I saw what he was laughing about. My mom! Surely hiking doesn't turn women into men, does it?

Gavin told me he was going on a Tararua Range walk one weekend soon.

"Poor you," I said.

I spent the weekend with Dad again and it was worse than

31

it always is. But one good thing came of it. It gave me the inspiration for my next letter to Lesley.

Dear Lesley,

Your letter about your dad made me thoughtful. He sounds to me as though he needs another wife, someone who'll understand him and clean up after his parties so you don't have to do it.

The trouble for me is having two parents who live separately, so I have to have completely different lifestyles for each one. When your father finds a girlfriend he should make sure she moves in with him so you don't have the problem of going to different houses on different weekends. Mom tends to say, "Go off and get out of my hair," because I'm with her most of the time. My dad mumbles about how we must have something called "quality time," and yet I hardly ever see him when I stay there. He's too busy with his politics to have much time for me.

You'll see what I mean more if I explain what happened this weekend. I've just spent it with Dad. He promised to take me flying a kite on Sunday morning. Now, he never used to be the sort who'd spend Sunday morning racing around with a kite. When I said, "Let's not bother," because I was happy watching Amanda's video, he got really angry and said of course I wanted to go. So I went, and all the way in his car he kept telling me about kites he'd made when he was a kid. And he rattled on about strawberry jelly bombs he made when he was a thing called a youngster, when kids played all day long and never lazed around watching TV. They never seemed to have parents then, either.

When we started flying the kite he got the string tangled around his windbreaker zipper, then the kite came down in some thorny bushes and we both got ripped to shreds retrieving it. Then it went up and Dad ran madly with it, shouting, "Look Henry, it's up!" with such desperate relief that he

32

forgot where he was and ran smack into the barrier they've put up to mark the end of the parking lot. He doubled over, moaning and clutching his balls, and when I said, "I'm sorry," he told me to go to hell.

It's very weird having a dad like that.

I hope you are OK.

I asked Mom if she was saving for my university tuition and she said she is going to sell me when I'm sixteen. If the price is right, maybe your dad will buy me.

Your pen pal,
Harassed Henry

I biked down to the post office immediately and mailed the letter.

9

The very next day Mom's new enthusiasm got under way. She phoned someone in the Hiking Club who recommended she start with a family hike that Sunday. You know what that means? Whenever it's a family do, I have to show up, never her sister or brother, or her parents in Invercargill. No. It's always me. If she didn't have me she wouldn't be able to go to lots of things. She says we're a family. I say we're too small to be a family. Families fill Honda Civics and play cricket on the beach at Christmas. Mom says we're a select, special family. I think that's rot.

To practice, she walked up Mount Victoria, the steepest hill in Wellington. She's probably the only person ever to have done it since the road was put in. I'm sure people thought she was a drunk driver who'd lost her license. Mom says cars are unecological. They poison the air. I say we should be grateful for technology. I bet Mom wouldn't like to do the washing with an old mangle and get water from the stream every time she wanted to water down her brandy. She's so irrational.

And, worst horror of horrors, Mom wanted to spend the May break at the Forest and Bird Lodge on Mount Ruapehu, a real mountain, right in the middle of nowhere as mountains always are. We weren't even members of the Forest and Bird Society. When she told me about this plan the scene went something like this:

I'm just coming in from Scouts. I hate Scouts but she makes me go. I'm taking my ridiculous scarf and slide off and she yells, "Is that you, Henry?"

34

"Yes." (Who else would throw a slide and scarf across the kitchen as they crept into my bedroom?)

"Good. Come here. I'm in bed. I want to talk to you."

I run through the possibilities: Dad's coming back. Mom's got cancer. Supercushion's been run over. Mrs. Matthews came around.

"It's about our May vacation, Henry."

"Yeah."

"Sit down. On the bed."

I sit down.

"I'd like you to come with me to the Forest and Bird Lodge at Mount Ruapehu for three nights."

"To do what?"

"To hike and observe birds and study the ecology of the place, and maybe to meet some interesting people."

"Oh no! Mom, I hate vacations away!"

"But, Henry, it's for you. You need new experiences and—"

"I don't! Anyway, I find mountains boring. Has this Lodge got TV?"

"No."

"Well, that's definite. I'm not going."

"But you'll enjoy it when you get there. You always do."

"I don't. I've never been there. I hate it."

"How do you know you'll hate it? Of course you will, with that attitude."

"There! There's no point in going then!"

"Henry. Please. I wish you liked birds and natural things . . ." Her voice just trailed off.

"I do. I like electricity. That's natural. TV and computers and movies and remote-control stuff."

"Henry! Stop it! I can't bear it! Please enjoy this vacation for—"

"No. You're always organizing my life. I want to choose a vacation I want. I'm not coming on this one!"

I got up, slammed her door, and went to my bedroom. I told Spanzini all about it. He agreed with me that Mom should let me choose a vacation for a change. I got into bed and snapped the light off.

I could hear Mom crying through the wall. Mom crying! I hadn't heard her crying since about a week before Dad left. I thought she'd cheered up after he'd gone. She said she wanted him to go. I was sure I hadn't been too awful in the argument. I turned over and put my old *Star Wars* pillow over my head to muffle the noise, but I could still hear it. I decided to be real nice and go and cheer her up. At least then I'd be able to sleep.

I sat on her bed and fed her tissues and said ''I'm sorry'' about ten times till she stopped crying.

''It's not you, Henry. Don't be sorry.''

''I'm sorry.''

Then she suddenly turned angry. ''Shut up! Why can't I be miserable without you having to be sorry all the time?''

''I'm—I mean—I don't know.''

''I'm sorry, Henry. I'm just having a self-pity session. It's so hard planning a vacation when you can't count on another adult coming.''

''What about Jill?''

''She's going to the South Island with Lionel next week.''

''Oh. I'll go to Ruapehu, Mom. It's OK.''

''No, Henry. You mustn't let me push you into things.''

''Oh, OK then. I won't go, Mom.''

She started crying even more. I went back to bed with my *Star Wars* pillow and my old Garfield pillow as well.

I woke up really early the next morning and decided I'd share the horror of the previous evening with Lesley. I sat up in bed and wrote furiously till Mom yelled at me to get up.

Dear Lesley,
You have no idea how lucky you are to have a dad who doesn't
want to go on vacation. Vacations are so boring. I hate the
long car journey. Does your dad make you sit in the back?

My mom wants us to go up to the Forest and Bird Lodge
at Mount Ruapehu for the May break. Can you imagine any-
thing so dreadful? And it's a volcano. It could blow up any
minute! That's the trouble with parents: they're always or-
ganizing your life. Imagine what an uproar there'd be if I
tried to organize Mom's life!

Do you play soccer? I used to. I know someone who has a
computer. His name is Gavin. He's in my gang.
Cheers,
Henry

Not a great letter, but it got something off my chest. I
mailed it on the way to school. I asked Mary how long it'd
take to get to Auckland. She said maybe two days, maybe
three. Then she said, "You mailed one just a couple of days
ago, Henry!"

"Yes."

"This pen pal sounds a good idea for you, Henry."

"Yes," I agreed, "I guess it does."

10

The day before the family walk, it rained. I lay on the teddy bears most of the time, conserving my energy and talking to Spanzini. He was bugging me about my New Year's Resolutions.

"Peace and quiet?" he whirred in my ear.

"Yes, well," I admitted, "there's been less peace and quiet this year than ever before."

"NYR2. Get rich?"

"So far only $2.50 writing stories for kids in my class. No possibility of expanding the business. Too many goody-goodies, like Rachel, who'd tell on me. And it was hard work!"

"And NYR3?"

"Well, maybe I'd better cross that one off, Spanzini. I'm beginning to realize that anyone Mom likes won't help me achieve peace and quiet or get rich. If only I could introduce her to the right sort of businessman."

"Henry! Go and see if the paper's come," Mom interrupted.

It was five o'clock. When I brought the *Post* around Mom was getting the wet washing off the line. She looked sour and as though she was in a hurry, which was crazy. It was Saturday, after all.

"Henry, could you nip over to Joe-across-the-road's and borrow some sugar? I've run out and we're having apple crumble with dinner. One of the Hiking Club members is coming. Hurry up! Off you go! Stop gawping! What I did to get you I'll never know."

My mom's total absence of sex education worries me. Thank goodness we have it at school now. I'll have to leave some of my exercise books around for her to read.

"Oh, and Henry, thank Joe for looking in on you tonight. I'm going out after dinner."

Gawd, I hate that. I must be too old to be babysat.

I got the sugar and told Joe not to bother about babysitting. I lied about someone else coming around. He shrugged and went back to his beer and the cricket on TV. So I had an unsupervised evening ahead.

Mom ordered me around—don't chew gum, change your sweater, can't you be helpful, set the table—all the time until the guy from the Hiking Club arrived. Then she was all nice. She told him I was a "good little soul." I think I'll stay up and watch late TV to get even with her.

We had soybean loaf for dinner. It was really disgusting. The hiker ate it all up. I got indigestion partly from the food but partly due to my perilous closeness to a nervous collapse. I could tell Mom was interested in this guy in an unnatural sort of way. She was acting like you do when you've pinned something on someone's back and you're trying to get them to realize something's up.

And this wasn't the professional type of man I wanted as a substitute dad. He didn't have a tie on, just a shirt and sweater. He had big rough hands too, no good for handling money. He was no use for NYR2 or NYR3. I decided to eliminate him.

After dinner Mom went to get ready and the bean-eating hiker and I sat in the living room pretending to watch TV.

"Did you know I have a rare inherited disease?" I asked him, very confidentially.

"No," he said. "You look pretty healthy to me."

"Well, I have zoolamionothropia actually. It's a gradual and agonizing liquefying of the backbone. It's all through my

39

mom's family. They can trace it right back to the jellyfish in prehuman times.''

''Oh,'' he said. Just ''Oh.'' I think he was too stunned to comment more.

''It seems, the specialist doctors tell us, that some humans descended from apes and stuff and an unfortunate few descended from jellyfish. Well, that lot is my mom's family. Her spine's just started to go actually. But she keeps a stiff upper lip and wears a stainless steel corset. I mean, what more can you do?''

''Oh, yeah?'' he said, standing up and leaning against the mantelpiece. ''Fancy that, eh.''

He seemed to me like one of those strong silent types who don't say much because they're stupid, but maybe he was just very sensitive, quite moved by this tragic tale.

Mom came in, smelling of some cream stuff. She hugged me and told me to go to bed and read and be sensible about putting my light out. After the door had slammed shut and they'd gone down the path laughing, the house felt very empty and I felt kind of sad. I was tempted to just put the light out and block out all the emptiness, but I didn't. I got out Lesley's letters and I reread the details about his father.

11

The Sunday evening after the hike, when I lay exhausted on my quilt, my legs seemed to keep walking all by themselves. But my mind! Oh boy, my mind was in overdrive. There was only one thing to do. I wrote and told Lesley all about it.

Dear Lesley,
I've gone right off women and I don't think men and women are a very good combination. Read on. You'll see why.

There we were, driving to the Tararua Ranges, when I suddenly saw Gavin Andrews grinning at me out of a huge car that overtook us on a bend and forced Mom into the gravel.

"Bloody male driver," she growled.

I'm psychic. That moment was when I knew the day would be a disaster.

Imagine this—Mom bending down to undo the rope that ties the car trunk shut, bending down in pink shorts, the same pink shorts she wore biking. They've got a gray shiny glow on them where the saddle was. And if that's not bad enough, it was in a public parking area with lots of other people about, including Gavin, his dad who's a businessman and, I'm sure, more sensitive than other sorts of men, and Rachel from school. She's a friend of Gavin's family, I think, and they brought her (which is crackpot, as everyone knows hiking makes men out of the people who do it).

Well, I couldn't let Gavin see Mom bending down in her shorts so I stood right behind her. But I couldn't let Gavin see me hunched up behind my mom either, so I stood behind her shading my eyes from the gray clouds and gazing at a distant peak with an outdoor look on my face.

It was all OK till there was this blast on a car's horn beside us. Mom screamed and leaped up and yelled, "What the bloody—" and then she shrieked, "Toot toot, you brute!" and this idiot, the bean-eating hiker from last night, clambered out of the car, all hairy arms and legs, like a spider. I didn't watch him and Mom for a while, but I heard her yell, "I'll try anything once!" and I knew Gavin heard too. He didn't look up from the complicated business of lacing up his proper hiking boots. Rachel was doing the same thing, only more neatly. Gavin's dad was doing something important, bending over the tailgate of their car.

I wandered over to them. Gavin and Rachel ignored me, probably because I had old sneakers on. Rachel looked as though she didn't want to go on the walk, or maybe she didn't want to walk with Gavin.

"Hey, Gavin," I said. "You want to hear about an explosion my father used to make when he was at school?"

"Oh, yeah?" said Gavin. Rachel just stared at my shoes. Gavin's dad called to him to go and help, and Gavin just walked away, head down. I yelled after him, "Bet you don't know how to make a jelly bomb!" Then I saw that Gavin's dad had a sort of helpless look on his face and I seized the opportunity to get something useful out of the day. I'd been thinking, on the ride over, about my dad's way of staying with a problem till he solved it. I didn't think I'd been trying hard enough with NYR2 and this seemed a good chance.

Mr. Andrews was unpacking a little camping stove.

"How did you make all your money, Mr. Andrews?"

He just laughed and got me to hold the stove while he stuffed a pipe-cleaner thing down a little tube on it. I couldn't believe a rich man would do things like that. It was the sort of thing Dad did in his workshop.

"Which is the best interest-bearing account, Mr. Andrews?"

"You making money, eh, lad?"

"Yes. I got—" and then I realized I couldn't tell him about my school writing business so I asked him if he had any jobs. He looked at me then, and said he might have a delivery component in a new venture about to be launched. I swear it. That's what he said. OK, it didn't make any sense, but I thought I'd show him how reliable and level-headed I was that day and maybe I'd get the job. He's very rich so he must pay good wages. I held the stove carefully and he wiped it and my hands with an oily rag.

"Henry! We're off now!"

Mom and the hairy bean-eating spiderman hiker were standing right beside us as we crouched on the grass.

Mr. Andrews looked up Mom's leg. "Hello, Suzy Jollifer, isn't it? Hi, Mark."

It turned out that Mark, the hairy bean-eating spiderman, worked for Mr. Andrews. They all stood like A-frames with their feet apart and their arms folded across their chests. God, the walk hadn't even started, and Mom was already copying the way the men did things. They all decided to walk up the track together.

We started off. I raced ahead to get away from Mom, but she seemed to think the walk was like a road race, and she tore up after me with the hairy spiderman swinging along silently behind her, and Mr. Andrews behind him.

Gavin and Rachel had gotten a head start on all of us. Rachel seemed to want to be by herself and Gavin wanted to get ahead of her so he could leap out of bushes and scare her. Rachel turned out to be a real know-it-all about birds and ferns and stuff and she was taller than Gavin and me. You don't notice that sort of thing when you sit next to someone in class. Maybe she had built-up boots on, or maybe she

43

was becoming a man. When I caught a glimpse of them ahead I slowed down, and Mom, gasping and saying "Oops" and "Oh, isn't it marvelous?" over and over, stepped on the back of my sneaker. The sixth time this happened I had to plunge into the bush to let the two men pass while I fixed my shoe. They strode past, talking about some new computerized accounts procedure for the office. Mom collapsed in a heap beside me. I had to heave her back up. She was laughing and really enjoying herself till she looked up the track and saw they hadn't waited. They were clearly so deeply involved in their talk that they hadn't even noticed Mom's temporary collapse, but she didn't seem to understand this. Boy, did she stop laughing. Her face was now the color of her shorts.

"Men!" she cursed.

"But Mom, it's the track, not the men! You can't blame them."

We plodded on together, and if I got too far ahead she yelled, "Coooo-eeeee! Henry!" We were on a zigzag and all the others were just above us. They could hear everything. In the circumstances I couldn't possibly give the mountain my best. What must Mr. Andrews have thought? If the job involves steep hills he'll never pick me now.

The worst moment of the climb was when Mom did Indian calls to me through the bush when she thought I'd got lost and I was actually having a piss. After that I knew my chances with Mr. Andrews were ruined. And I wouldn't be in Gavin's gang anymore.

I let Mom go in front. She'd quieted down a lot, but now I had to look at her huge pink shorts all the time. No wonder I never saw a single kiwi. She was walking almost bent double, grasping at roots and branches, hauling herself along.

When we got to the flat place near the top everyone else was having lunch. Mr. Andrews had the hot water boiling. Rachel was at the top of a pine—goodness knows how she got there—throwing cones down to Gavin, who was kicking

44

them off the edge of this cliff. I must say Rachel has stamina. Surely that much of it isn't natural for girls, is it, Lesley?

I sat down behind a flax bush and Mom flung herself down beside Mark and Mr. Andrews, who were talking about cricket now. That was the most peaceful time of the whole day. But Mark gave Mom a cup of tea and she perked up immediately.

"Henry! Come and get a sandwich. You're too old for hide-and-seek!"

Another humiliation. Then another followed. She'd brought whole-wheat sandwiches with mashed kidney beans spread on them. She offered them to everyone and no one wanted one. God, I couldn't look. I scraped a hole between my knees with a pinecone. Mark offered me some peanut butter and jam on white bread and I thanked him. He looked at me and we shared a moment of understanding about Mom. She was furious. You should have seen the way she ate all the whole-wheat sandwiches with her jaws really revving. And the way she leaped up after that, when Gavin and Mark and Mr. Andrews and I were all discussing sports, and started organizing swims in the creek!

"Too cold," Mr. Andrews said very firmly.

"Yeah. Only jellyfish would swim in that," Mark said.

"What?" laughed Mom.

My blood ran cold. I scuttled behind the flax bush again.

Mark lay back into the space I'd just left, stared up at the clouds, and laughed. "That boy of yours, he told me you were descended from jellyfish and you wear a steel corset!"

I was lying flat behind the bush now and the ground vibrated with Mr. Andrews's and Mark's belly laughs.

Mom got up and stood over Mark. I could see her shadow. "Henry said what?"

Mark seemed to be rolling around laughing.

"Do I look as though I wear a steel corset?" she shrieked.

This made them laugh even more. Gavin was laughing too. And I heard Rachel tittering in the tree. She was up so far she could look down and see me. I'd never be able to go to school again.

"All right then. I'm not scared of a bit of cold water!" And Mom strode down the slope to the creek and just jumped in, fully clothed.

That was bad enough, but when she came up and everyone could see the outline of her breasts, I, well, I ran and hid. She told me later she jumped up and down—thank goodness I didn't watch—to get warm, and that no one offered her a bush shirt or anything. Of course she had nothing dry to put on, so I had to walk back down with her all wet like that. I was almost dead with embarrassment by the time we got to the parking lot. She didn't want to chat to any of her fellow club members who, strangely enough, were way behind. She just jabbed the starter and we shot off.

She told me in the car they were all sanctimonious idiots who wouldn't know a cabbage tree from a cauliflower if they weren't labeled. Wow—was she cross! I tried to make her see it was all her fault, and she became a danger on the road.

Well, it's nearly midnight and the flashlight battery's fading. I know my dad would disapprove of my breaking a resolution but I've decided Mom's better without men, and they're better without her. Goodbye, NYR3.

Bye, Lesley,
Henry

12

Spanzini does his thinking slowly, by Earth standards. It took him till 3:30 on Tuesday afternoon to work out his little scheme, and he didn't tell me until I was lying on the couch, with Supercushion crushing my rib cage, half watching how to count to eleven with Big Bird on TV and half trying to write another story for Gavin. I'd increased my price to a dollar.

"Henry, are you receiving me?" I heard this little voice say in my ear.

"Spanzini! What brings you to our dimension, space traveler?"

"I have a plan, a plan that could result in the successful accomplishment of your NYR1."

"Yeah?"

"And NYR2!"

"Yeah!"

"And NYR3!"

"What!"

And then Spanzini told me his simple but brilliant plan. I immediately sent Supercushion flying across the room, sat down at the kitchen table, and wrote the fateful letter, the letter that could change my life. I didn't hint. I spread my idea right out in the open. I know that's the right technique when you've finally had an idea that no one has ever thought of before.

Dear Lesley,
How about you persuading your dad to take a blood-pressure-

*lowering vacation at the Forest and Bird Lodge, Mount Rua-
pehu! It's halfway between Auckland and Wellington, just off
Highway One, so it's a good place to meet. We could get to
know each other properly and our parents could meet and
fall in love and marry and we'd have the same father and
mother! You'd have a more interesting life with my mom having enthusiasms. (She's bound to be off natural foods by then.)
And I'd have the routine, respectability, and solid financial
background I need.*

What do you say?

*We'd have to plant the idea in our parents' heads, about
meeting a choice new partner on this trip, otherwise they
might not notice each other. But I'm sure we can organize
it. People usually fall in love with no help from kids. So it's
bound to be that much easier if we're there to encourage it.*

Write, fax, or phone me immediately when you get this.
Henry

*PS   I've always wanted a brother. I'd go to your school and
I wouldn't have to sit next to a sissy girl anymore!*

I mailed it straightaway. Thank goodness the post office
was just down the road. Probably Lesley's post office is several miles down his private drive, then half an hour's ride in
a Ferrari.

I waited for the whole of the next day, paralyzed with sus-
pense. Mom kept nagging me to clean the bathroom and my
bedroom.

Then I realized Lesley wouldn't even have gotten my letter
by then! I spent the next few days in a trance. I went around
to Gavin's on Sunday. He'd taken up smoking and wanted a
lookout person. Seeing him choking and spluttering took my
mind off Lesley's letter for a bit. Of course I didn't tell Gavin
any of it.

Next Tuesday, after school, I got an airmailed reply from

Lesley. This was too private to read under the walnut tree, so I locked myself in the bathroom and tore open the envelope.

Dear Henry,

I'm word processing this in my study instead of doing my homework. Dad'll be furious if he comes in and finds me writing to you instead of doing my Rocky Shore project. So this must be quick. In short—I agree with your proposal.

My agreement means: I pledge to get my father—by fair means or foul—to the Forest and Bird Lodge, Ruapehu, for the May break.

I have drawn up a contract between you and me stating our commitment. There are two copies. Would you please read it, sign both copies, keep one for your records, and send one back to me for mine. I have signed them both, in blood.

Please note: the consequence of breaking the contract shall be—banishment from the other person's mailbox in perpetuity.

I can't write more now. See you in May, or else.

Lawyer Lesley

There I was, standing in that dingy old bathroom that Mom had "brightened up" with purple paint one wet weekend last year. I remember Dad had described the color as "the last straw." There I was, surrounded by this bad taste, staring at the beautiful laser-printed contract that I held in my trembling right hand. My left hand clasped the thick blue envelope. I was temporarily overcome.

I flushed the toilet, from habit, and slowly and dreamily walked through the kitchen. I noticed with disgust that no one had done the breakfast dishes. I noticed that the cold tap was dripping. I noticed that there was a fly on the edge of Supercushion's bowl.

I moved out of the house, along the mean, damp concrete path to the front of my ancestral home. I stared at our small weatherboard one-story place with its peeling paintwork, bulging garbage cans, and the perfectly ordinary Yale keyhole. Everyone else is getting burglar-proof big brass ones.

Now, at last, I knew I had the power to change all this. I called Spanzini to my shoulder. I whispered the good tidings to him.

"Henry, my old son," he said, "you shall have riches heaped upon you. You shall have a father powerful and loving, stern yet devoted—who will die soon of a massive heart attack, leaving you to take over his financial empire. You, the youngest entrepreneur in New Zealand's history. A young man in the right place at the right time."

"Henry! Bring me the bloody paper and don't just stand there gawking like a twit. Henry!"

As I struggled past the weeds down the path to the gate to get the *Post,* I gazed fondly and with nostalgia at the tumbledown garden, the cracked concrete path, the leaning garden shed, the collapsing picket fence, and the dented yellow Mini parked outside. I had the letter and contracts under my T-shirt.

Mom grabbed the paper and spread it over the table—our only table—and started looking for the Entertainments pages. A parent who's doing his or her job well would look for the Business pages to see how to invest for their child's future.

"Yep! It's on!" she yelled at me as she phoned Jill. For a whole week after the hike Mom had been very grumpy. She'd blamed me for all sorts of things I couldn't do anything about, like the car overheating and Supercushion being off his food. But on Monday Jill had gotten back early from her South Island holiday and she'd phoned Mom and they'd roared like lions all evening. When Mom had crashed the receiver down she'd burst into my bedroom and said, "Jill left him in the

Homer Tunnel with a flat tire,'' and then she'd skipped into the kitchen and made us both cocoa and popcorn.

So I wasn't surprised that she and Jill were going to the movies in the middle of the week. What did surprise me was Jill and Mom falling into each other's arms and wheezing and honking with laughter on the doorstep, and Mom dashing off without even making sure I wasn't going to let in burglars and child molesters by the dozen in her absence.

At last I had peace and quiet. I lay on the teddy bears, unfolded the two legal contracts and—the phone rang.

13

It was Dad. He wanted to speak to Mom. When I said she wasn't in, he wanted to know who was looking after me and where Mom had gone. I told him a folk dancing school-teacher and a hairy bean-eating hiker were sitting on the couch looking after me while my backbone turned to jelly in front of them. He told me it was a serious matter to leave children on their own, so I told him he'd done it well and truly. That got him out of the bossy parent mood. He said he'd phone hourly till Mom returned, and I pointed out that he'd wake me up.

"Oh," he said. "How are you doing at school these days, Henry?"

"Brilliantly, Dad. I've put your name on the list of parents with hobbies they can teach in our electives next term."

"What?"

"Yes. For kite flying and explosive making."

He groaned and hung up, and I could get back to Lesley's letter and the contract.

I read it slowly. It was in strange language but I could just understand it.

CONTRACT

This contract, made the first day of April

| BETWEEN | *Lesley Lacey* |
| AND | *Henry Jollifer* |

WHEREAS *Lesley Lacey is the child of Conrad Lacey, of Seacliffs, St. Mary's Bay, Auckland, lawyer, and*

WHEREAS *Henry Jollifer is the son of——Jollifer of 24 Hardy St., Wellington, of unknown employment,*

AND WHEREAS *Lesley Lacey and Henry Jollifer wish that Conrad Lacey and——Jollifer should meet*

NOW *this deed witnesseth as follows:*

In consideration of Lesley Lacey's agreement to ensure the presence of Conrad Lacey at the Forest and Bird Lodge, Ruapehu, New Zealand, on a date to be arranged during the May vacation, Henry Jollifer agrees to ensure the presence of——Jollifer at the Forest and Bird Lodge, Ruapehu, New Zealand.

In consideration of Henry Jollifer's agreement to ensure the presence of——Jollifer at the Forest and Bird Lodge, Ruapehu, New Zealand, on a date to be arranged during the May vacation, Lesley Lacey agrees to ensure the presence of Conrad Lacey at the Forest and Bird Lodge, Ruapehu, New Zealand.

Signed by the said Lesley Lacey at Auckland, this first day of April

Lesley Lacey
WITNESS (scribble)

Signed by the said Henry Jollifer at Wellington this——day of——

WITNESS (left blank)

I was very impressed. Lesley had obviously inherited legal skills from his dad. I couldn't work out why my mom's name was dash Jollifer or why Lesley was the child of Conrad and I was the son of dash Jollifer. But I knew that, with Mr. Lacey and Lesley teaching me law, I'd be a whiz at contracts in a day or so.

It was really dark and I'd forgotten to draw my curtains. The windows looked like new blackboards with nothing written on them, not even today's date at the top. That gave me a choice idea. I climbed onto the kitchen bench and opened the high-up kitchen cupboards that Mom never uses. That's where I keep my stash of loot that Mom doesn't know about. I've got a cigarette lighter (from Gavin), lots of coupons for ten cents off supermarket items, a photo of Amanda she gave me and I didn't want Mom to see (Dad's got his arm around her and she looks much happier than Mom did when Dad had his photo taken with her), a cartridge from a real bullet that must have really been fired at something, some shaving cream I stole from Dad in case I suddenly need it one day and it's a Sunday and the shops are shut, and a jar of glue labeled "Room 5."

I took the shaving cream aerosol can and the creamy white glue out of the cupboard and jumped down to the floor. My imagination was being guided by Spanzini. He was whispering into my right ear as I mixed the shaving cream and glue together in our salad bowl. Mom told me once she'd gotten it as a wedding present, so it must be ancient and obsolete.

"Henry, you must practice your signature on the blackboard so you can sign the deed and your checks."

"Checks, Spanzini?"

"Checks, Henry. You'll use so many of them the bank will give you a hardback checkbook."

I took the sticky white mixture into my bedroom and placed it carefully on the teddy bear quilt. Then I sat beside it and practiced my signature in the air, like little kids do in first grade. I got it just right and carefully transferred it to my window blackboard.

Spanzini told me to add lots of squiggles underneath it. I was busy doing this when there was a knock at the door! A child molester, maybe! It turned out to be Joe-across-the-road, who'd seen the signature and wanted to know why I was making Christmas decorations in autumn. I think he must have been lonely and was just coming over for a chat. He sure chatted a lot as we tried to scrub the glue off the windows. The scrubbing was his idea. He reckoned Mom wouldn't like the signature. This surprised me. I hadn't given Mom a thought. But I was in a mellow mood after Lesley's wonderful letter and I decided to go along with Joe-across-the-road—just to keep the mood sweet.

After Joe had left, I signed the contract—in bright red pen. I hoped Lesley would think it was a modern type of high-class blood.

14

All I then had to do was persuade Mom to take a vacation at the Forest and Bird Lodge. That wouldn't be hard to do as she already wanted to go there. Yippee! NYR3 resolving coming up!

The next night, when I was doing the dishes and Mom was reading the paper, I asked her: "Mom, did you book the Forest and Bird Lodge like you planned?"

She rattled her paper, then flung it down. "That subject is now closed, Henry, closed." She picked up a dishtowel and started polishing the plates. "And I want you in bed early tonight, please. Brent from the Organic Food Co-op is coming around."

Gawd. Who is Brent? I thought. And what if Mom's planning to marry him? There was obviously no time to lose.

"Mom, I just want to know about the Forest—"

"The subject is C-L-O-S-E-D!"

I did the rest of the dishes with my mind in a spin.

When Mom kissed me good night I tried to bring the subject up again.

"Mom?"

"Yes, dear."

"I think I really like mountains, you know that?"

"Huh? I've never seen any evidence of it."

"Mom?"

"Yes, dear?"

"I want to go to a mountain this vacation."

"Do you," she said, without any expression, as she tucked me in.

"Yes, a big mountain, with a real crater and forests and birds and things. Don't you?"

"Do I? No! I told you to quit yapping about the vacation."

"Sorry, Mom."

"And stop whining about being sorry. Good night!"

She switched off the light and closed the door into the kitchen.

Dear Lesley,
I'm writing by flashlight under my Garfield pillow. It casts a golden light. Mom won't listen to me about the trip. I've signed the contracts but I have to get a witness. It shouldn't be hard, I guess. How did you get yours?

It's going to be a hard job getting Mom there. Hope your dad's easier to arrange.
Yours,
Henry

This letter must have crossed at our post office with one from Lesley, which arrived two days later, on Friday.

Dear Henry,
I have problems. With the very snoopy cleaning lady and the housekeeper. It's very hard to hide your letters. A few days ago I put all your letters in a carved box beside my bed. I came in to find the cleaning lady starting to read them. I screamed at her and grabbed them. Now I'm taking them to school daily, and I'm going to keep them in my violin case when I'm at home. I can hear if someone's opening that and taking my violin out.

But it's a hassle. I live on tenterhooks. Bad for the nerves. What if someone finds them at school when they're busy

*stealing my lunch? I could be blackmailed. Be warned. Keep
your letters safely hidden from your cleaning lady and your
mother.*
Yours in league,
Lesley

Our cleaning lady was dyeing her hair red in the bathroom
sink while I was reading this. She—my mom—was splashing
dye all over the wall and floor and on the towel. I know this
because she called me in twice to hand her a dropped towel.
She said she didn't dare open her eyes or else they'd go red
too. I couldn't stop her wanting red hair. I just hoped that
Lesley's father liked red hair.

I'd had a hard day at school and home and it was quite
nice having more time to myself while Mom was in the bathroom. It meant I could write a really long letter to Lesley,
and boy, did I have a lot to tell him!

Dear Lesley,
*If only you knew what lengths I had to go to to get a witness
to the contract. I guess I could tell you. Here goes:*

*In Reading yesterday I thought I'd get Gavin to be my
witness because he's in the Cool Cougars reading group—
that's the slowies—and he wouldn't be on to legal documents
yet. But the Cool Cougars had to read a play for the whole
class and Gavin had to be the wolf. He was in a real bad
mood.*

*I couldn't ask him at lunchtime either, because I'm not in
his gang anymore. I told him I was resigning the day after
the hike. Better to resign than be made redundant, I'd heard
Joe-across-the-road telling Mom one day. "Always bloody
do it to them first," he'd said. Anyway, I was hanging around
the bike sheds, still trying to catch the flat tire creep, when
Mrs. Matthews called me over. She was on duty. You can tell*

when teachers are on duty. They stand all hunched up with both hands wrapped around a cup of tea.

"Henry, I've phoned your mother. She's popping over after school for a chat."

That's a disadvantage of a mom like mine. Your dad must be far too busy to be popping in and out of your school when he wants a chat.

I was pretty depressed in PE and Rachel made it worse. When I was lining up for a sprint I heard her telling some other girls about me running down that bush track after Mom. God, she's awful. She just giggles all the time. Gavin's really good at PE so he was in a better mood, and when we got into our math groups and he and I were working on the same problems, he even suggested that we do half each and then swap answers.

"OK," I said, "if you sign my will," and I took the contract out of my sweatshirt and unfolded it enough for him to sign.

"OK," he said, "but only if you show me how to make a jelly bomb."

"OK," I said, "but only a diagram."

"OK," he said, and we did the gang's handshake.

Mom was late coming home. I was getting hungry, then I remembered. Jeez, what must they be talking about!

I pedaled back to school and sneaked up along the side of our classroom. The windows just above my head were open and I could hear what was going on inside the room.

First shock. "Well, it's not how we did it in my day," said my father. *Dad! What was he doing at school? Was Mrs. Matthews acting as a marriage guidance counselor?*

Mrs. Matthews whispered something, then she must have come over to the window and looked out. She couldn't have seen me up against the uncomfortable weatherboards.

"I'm so sorry to hear about your separation," she said. "It must be hard for Henry."

Silence. Maybe Mom wasn't there. Then, "He's OK, Henry is." That was Mom, sort of mumbling.

"Well," said Mrs. Matthews, "that may be, but he's become overconscientious at school. Er, does he socialize at all?"

What did she mean? Surely not—then Mom interrupted, which was more normal.

"He's very active. We went on a hike with Gavin and Rachel the Sunday before last."

I shut my eyes and saw Mrs. Matthews's round-as-a-record mouth again.

"Oh. I wondered. He seems very awkward with girls. Being an only child, I imagine—"

"I know what you mean," said Dad. "I've got four sisters."

"Yeah, and look at your attitude to women," snapped Mom.

What if they had a fight in front of Mrs. Matthews? I jammed myself under the windowsill.

"He plays with Gavin a lot," Mom said.

"Oh, yes, Gavin Andrews. A nice boy," said Mrs. Matthews.

Then the second shock happened to my already shattered system. I heard running feet on the grass, and someone yelling, "Over there! Knew we'd find a sucker."

I turned, and Gavin and his new gang were charging across the playground with a huge red cake thing—with candles—no! no! it couldn't be—

BANG!!!!!!

And then I was on the ground with my ears feeling so big I thought I'd turned into an elephant. I tried to open an eye but all I could see was blood gluing my eyelids shut. So—well—what would you have done? I guess anyone would have fainted. I passed out right there in a pool of sticky blood.

When I came to I was surrounded by stunned adults, and

gobs and blobs of strawberry jelly—not blood—-were every-where.

That was bad enough. Worse was the fact that I had to have a shower in the gym, and there was nothing wrong with me, and Dad had to help me get the gobs and blobs and glugs out of my hair and eyes and ears and nostrils and mouth.

Even though Gavin was suspended and I received an apol-ogy note from him, I shall never ever make a deal with him again.

I enclose your contract. Excuse the few red smears and seeds on it. Please let me know when you get it.

I'm sorry you're having trouble hiding my letters. My mom doesn't go through my room so I'm OK. Maybe you could put them under your mattress.

Hope you didn't have as much trouble as I did when you got your witness. Was your witness a girl? Looks a bit like it. Leonard, the new member of Gavin's gang, tells me they'll do anything if a boy asks them roughly enough. I guess it's legal to have girl witnesses. I'm not sure though. Maybe you'd better check that out with your dad. Probably it'd be more legal if it was a boy witness—more reliable, I mean.
Hopeful Henry

I had to end the letter quickly as Mom was phoning Dad. Maybe they were getting together again! I've read in the *Woman's Weekly* that parents sometimes do this when the welfare of their child is at stake.

"I'll kill him!" I heard her yell. Then there was a pause, then she slammed down the receiver.

"Dad wants you to go to boarding school!" she shouted. "That's a born-again socialist talking, Henry."

I will never understand my parents.

15

I waited a week for a reply to that letter and the one before that.

Dear Henry,
I didn't have too much trouble with a witness. While I was waiting for my violin teacher to finish with the child prodigy she teaches before me, I talked to the prodigy's seven-year-old older sister who's into practicing her signature in joined-up writing. I just put the contracts in front of her and said, "Sign here," and she did.

It's so easy to get what you want when you're a big full-back for the school rugby team, as I am. Little girls are scared of me. Maybe I haven't mentioned my rugby skills before. I'm in the first 15 as well as a Junior Auckland Rep for soccer. The practices make it hard for me to fit my customary boxing and karate workouts into my weekend schedule but I manage somehow. Do you like sports?

Thanks for the contract. It's funny to think it's traveled all the way from my house to yours, even to your school, and back to me, yet we've never met.

Well, must go to my warm-ups.
Machoman Lesley

I was lying under the walnut tree reading this, even though it was getting a bit too cold to sit under the tree after school. I must say I was a bit surprised by this letter. Lesley didn't sound the way he had before. I felt a bit inferior, just a teensy weensy bit. I mean, I didn't know anyone in a first 15 or even a last 15. Our school didn't have a first 15. However, I decided it'd be quite good to have a brother who was in one. He could bash up Gavin for me.

I wrote back the next day.

Dear Lesley,
Yes, I do like sports. I watch flat out every Saturday and Sunday. I prefer to take an overview of the whole game. That's why I watch rather than play. I guess it's like being a TV producer rather than just an actor.

My hiding place for letters is a headache at the moment. Mom discovered the fat brown envelope of them I'd put in my underwear drawer, but luckily I came in just in time to stop her reading them. She thought they were love letters! Imagine!! But then I moved them to a real smart place. You know her enthusiasm for folk dancing has petered out. Well, I put them behind a set of folk dancing books on the book-shelf. It's three large books in a cardboard carton thing. I was sure they'd be safe there. You know what? The next day Mom took a day off from work and she did a big cleanout. I came home just in time to rescue the envelope from the gar-bage can.

By the way, if our parents are to fall in love, hadn't we better find out what they like in the opposite sex? You know—clothes styles and perfumes, whatever makes people fall in love.
Yours,
Henry

PS Does your dad like red hair and a brunette forehead and neck?

I didn't get an answer to this letter immediately, which was worrying. Maybe Lesley was too busy with rugby and soccer to think about our project. But I kept sneaking looks

63

at the contract. I now kept it shelved with Mom's gardening books.

A week after I'd mailed the last letter to Lesley, I trapped Mom into a significant conversation while we were doing the dishes.

"Mom?"

"Yes, dear?"

"I've been thinking about the May break, and—"

"Don't start on that again! And hold your shoulders back when you're scrubbing the pots. I don't want to hear about vacation."

"But Mom, I have to do a school project during the break."

"A what!"

"A project. About volcanoes."

"Why? Why then, for goodness' sake?"

"Well, it's because I didn't finish it for the due date last week, and we've started on Fiji now and Mrs. Matthews said I have to complete the volcanoes project during the break."

"Why didn't you finish it? Mrs. Matthews told me you were working too hard!"

"Well, I need to visit a volcano, an extinct one, to get some pictures for my project folder and—"

"Oh, for crying out loud, Henry! Surely Mrs. Matthews doesn't expect me to take you to a bloody volcano for the May break just so you can finish your project. Are you going on a class trip to Fiji as well?"

"No, Mom, but, well, I want to do well in the vol—"

Mom was holding a cast-iron saucepan when I said that, and she looked at me strangely, opened her fingers, and dropped the pot on her foot.

In the waiting room at the Medical Center I had to put up with Mom's swear words blasting out from the surgery. I hoped no one knew me. I read two *Woman's Weekly*s from cover to cover. When Mom came out she hobbled over to me and boomed, "They can't bloody plaster a broken toe. Nothing, that's what that zombie said he could do about it! Nothing!''

I shot out the door into the street, my face red with humiliation.

At home I got Mom settled in the big chair in front of the TV with a bag of popcorn beside her, then I went into my room to write an urgent note to Lesley.

Dear Lesley,
Why haven't you answered my letter?
My mom's at home for a week with a broken toe. I have to wait on her night and day. I don't think she'll be able to go hiking in May. All is lost. I feel desperate. She's got a new enthusiasm now too. She's started watching TV, the wrong channel every time.
Henry

The next morning was Saturday and it was raining. I got a letter from Lesley. Our letters had crossed again in the mail.

Dear Henry,
I'm now able to reply because I have the results of my dad's sexual attractiveness profile. I took note of every woman who came to the house this week—except Grannie.
Six had light hair, not really blond. Four had dark hair. Two of the dark-haired ones had very curly hair. He seemed to like those two best, although it's hard to know with him as he never tells me anything. The blond one, who was measuring for carpets, had a nice bottom. I heard Dad say that to a man friend of his in the evening.
When I asked him what his ideal woman would look like, he said, "I don't mind the package; it's the person inside that counts." I asked what he didn't like about women and he said he didn't like loud women. And they have to be quite

tall. *"I can't stand peering down at little women."* Dad is
6'3".

*Your mom's not loud, is she? I imagine her as quiet and
fiercely determined, and very loving. Is that right? And how
tall is she?*
Yours,
Lesley

"Henry! Here a minute! Was there any mail?"

"No, Mom!" I bawled from the kitchen to her bedroom.
I had to bellow my lungs out because I was competing with
the rain on the corrugated-iron roof. How I long to live in a
house that has a quiet roof. Maybe it would quiet Mom.

"What were you reading as you came up the path then,
eh? Come in here!" Mom can shout really loudly without
even pulling a muscle in her broken toe.

I sighed. Mom showed no sign of getting up, but she was
as nosy as ever.

"No mail for you, I meant!"

"Ah! And who's yours from, eh?"

"No one. I mean, my pen pal."

"Ah! Aha! This girl—"

"It's *not* a girl!"

"Henry, come closer. Come in here. Why are you blush-
ing if it's not a girl? Henry? Sit down, sweetie."

I sat down on her bed.

"Get off my flamin' foot!" she bellowed.

I ran.

I thought hard about my NYR3 for the rest of the day. The
sheer impossibility of the problem! It would daunt some people like Gavin—people who have everything too easy. But
me, having to fight for everything I've got, and coping with
Mom's enthusiasms: well, I'm tough. Mr. Lacey has got to
be made to see past her gruesome imperfections to whatever
it is that makes her tick.

16

With Mom's height in her passport listed as 5'4" and with
her broken toe, and with only three weeks to go till the trip,
I knew it was going to be difficult to keep my part of the
deal. But—I had so much to gain: a rich dad, a secure inher-
itance, a computer, and a happier mom who didn't have to
work.

OK, so Mom was a bit short for Mr. Lacey. That was a
problem. I couldn't stretch her on an old-fashioned prewar
torture rack. I needed Spanzini.

"Spanzini. Hello, Spanzini. Come in, Spanzini."

"What zup?"

"Spanzini, how are you and how is your dimension?"

"Out of this world."

"Choice. Spanzini, could you expand your infinite imagination into super problem-solving mode?"

"SPSM ready to run."

"Good. Spanzini, how can I make Mom a foot taller?"

"There is a dimension that makes humans extrude like lic-
orice and—"

"Spanzini! No. It has to be on this earth."

"Ah. Could she keep her arms above her head, with a
periscope in her hands, to see over tall people?"

"No, Spanzini. She couldn't make my dinner like that, or
drive the car."

"Ah. What about the other end of her? Put blocks under
her feet? I have seen some women in shopping centers, and
all women at school prize givings, with these blocks under
their shoes."

"Spanzini! That's it! High heels! You're a genius!"

"Henry, please accept the compliments of my dimension. Goodbye till our next shared time frame."

I rolled off the flattened and stitched teddy bears, threw my *Star Wars* pillow across the room, and kicked my stuffed Garfield. I'd solved the impossible problem. Mom had old stiletto heels in the back of her cupboard. I used a pair once for a fancy dress. She could just wear those at the Forest and Bird Lodge. Of course, she'd have to be made to wear them, but I was sure I could persuade her.

But there was another impossible problem. Mom still wasn't intending to go on vacation at all. This depressed me, and no amount of lying on my horrible babyish bed squashing the teddy bears was going to solve it. I had many days of bleak hopelessness over this. The only thing that kept me going was remembering my dad's seriousness about resolutions. I knew I mustn't give up in this dark and difficult time.

Then, just when the teddy bears were looking as though they'd been flattened by a caterpillar tractor, Mom said something that gave me an idea. It was when we were doing the dishes. That's the time I always do my heavy talking to Mom.

"Mom?"

"Yes, dear? Don't use so much detergent and rinse them properly."

"Mom, about the May vacation. I've changed—"

"Henry! I told you I don't want to hear about it. You do what you want. I'll do what I want. We'll just forget about it being a family event."

"Mom?"

"What is it now? Do that jug. It's been on the bench for days."

"I'm sorry I said that stuff about the Forest and Bird Lodge."

"Shut up! I hate your being sorry about everything as well."

She went on drying the dishes for a while. I cleaned the jug till it sparkled, and I managed to get one huge bubble right across the top of it.

"Mom?"

"Yes, dear?"

"Will your foot need exercise to get better?"

"No. I never want to exercise again. I've begun to like lying in bed. Why?"

"Oh, nothing. I just wondered."

I went to my bedroom and consulted Spanzini. Spanzini thought I should look on the bright side and organize my own vacation, like Mom had said. He said it was "calling her bluff."

So—I did just that! The next day, with only twenty days to go until vacation started, I got home as soon as I could after school. I phoned the Forest and Bird Society. They explained you had to be a member of Forest and Bird before you could use the Lodge. Family membership cost twenty dollars. I biked down to the post office right away and got out all my savings—fifty dollars—and I stuck it in an envelope. I wrote a note to Forest and Bird explaining that I was enclosing the membership fee for a family, twenty dollars, and the cost of three nights' accommodation at the Forest and Bird Lodge. I sneaked another stamp from Mom's stash and mailed it. Easy! I felt like a managing director.

When Mom came home from work I made us both a cup of tea.

"How was your first day back after the accident?" I asked.

"Dreadful! The Xerox machine jammed. There was a leaving present collection for some joker on the next floor who I hardly know, and then there was a fire drill in the rain. I need a rest."

She looked a bit sad, sitting there in the chair, staring at nothing and stroking Supercushion automatically.

"Phone your dad up, love, and ask him if he can have you this weekend. I don't feel very good at the moment."

Mom doesn't often say that, but I hate it when she does. I feel like a throwaway circular that comes in the mail. I must have looked a bit hurt because she leaned over and gave me a big kiss on my ear and a hug. No wonder I'm such a social mess. Mom is so changeable. How can I know what's going on in her head?

"Henry, I know I'm being horrible at the moment. It's a combination of tiredness from work, the pain in the toe, and other things. Thanks for being nice."

I nearly dropped my cup then, but of course I didn't.

"You know, Henry, Supercushion's put on weight. I thought it was just growth, but now I'm not so sure. He might have an abscess. We'd better watch him closely. He's such a fighter."

We both stroked Supercushion, who shut his eyes tight and stared straight at us, purring.

"You didn't check the mailbox today, Henry. There's a letter from your girlfriend. It's on the bench."

I was shocked—shocked that Mom still persists in calling Lesley my girlfriend, but also shocked that I'd been so busy organizing the trip I'd forgotten to check the mail. I left Mom and Supercushion and took the blue envelope off to my bedroom where Spanzini and I could read it together.

Dear Henry,
I'm still waiting for a character analysis of your mom. Maybe her astrological sign would be useful too. And have you managed yet to get your mother committed to the trip? Hurry up! It's only three weeks away, two-and-a-half by the time you get this.

And I can't write so many letters now as I'm having problems getting stamps. I only get pocket money if I can file a return with Dad showing exactly how I've spent last week's amount. He then gives me another amount which is bigger or smaller depending on how wisely I've spent the last lot.

Last week I had to buy $3 worth of stamps and he queried it. He said my return for such excessive letter-writing wasn't lucrative enough to warrant this continued expenditure. He said that I should cut down!

So, in case I can never write again, we are booked into the Lodge in the second week of the vacation—Monday, Tuesday and Wednesday.

Get your act together. Show some initiative!

I must go and shave now and get ready for school. I keep thinking I'll grow a very long beard, then I get tired of the weight of it—it grows so quickly—and I shave it off. The housekeeper's always furious because it clogs the drain. My father's clean-shaven. Find out if your mother prefers that.
Lesley

Wow! His dad must be mean about money! I'll have to change his attitude when I'm more closely related to him.

Lesley shaves! I knew I was stunted and a slow developer. God!—what is he going to think of me when we meet! Maybe Mom and Lesley's dad will float off hand in hand and Lesley won't even speak to me!

17

Dad couldn't have me to stay that weekend because Amanda and he were going to some meeting in Auckland. But it turned out to be very fortunate that they were away. I'm almost sure Spanzini had something to do with it.

On Saturday the sun was shining and Mom got up at the normal time. Jill had been around the night before and Mom seemed to be in a cheerier mood. We were sitting around the kitchen table reading the *Listener* and the *Dominion* and eating toast. I was staring into the neighbor's garden, which you can look right into from our kitchen. I kept imagining Lesley finishing a game of rugby and being collected by a chauffeur and rushed off to a special soccer clinic coached by Diego Maredonna. I looked across at Mom, who was dressed in her old dungaree overalls and looking so ordinary. I mean, she could have been anyone's mom.

"I've never seen a bearded soccer player, have you, Mom?"

"What? What will you come out with next? Bearded soccer players! Is this a new school project?"

"D'you like bearded men, Mom?"

"I don't like any men at the moment, love, bearded or not."

"But if you did?"

"Well, yes, beards are quite nice. When I met your dad he had a beard."

"No!"

"Yes, and long hair."

"Oh yeah?"

"Yes. Down his back in a ponytail it was."

I was stunned out of my brain. My dad with a ponytail! And Mom falling for him! Adults are just so bizarre!

"Gawd, mustn't get nostalgic, must I, Henry?" she said, and she mussed up my hair, which I hate her doing. I particularly hate it when I'm eating toast. She nearly made me jab it up my nose.

"No. No use. Get the mail, sweetie. Your dad may have remembered to send me the check for your school camp fees for last term."

I went down the path to the box. No big blue envelope from Lesley, but there was one letter for me, from Forest and Bird. I put it on the table and went into my bedroom to offer a quick prayer to Spanzini. When I came back Mom waved the letter at me.

"It's for you. You must be getting old enough to have your name on unsolicited mailing lists. It's probably full of pictures of wretched penguin chicks."

I opened it. Inside was a form letter welcoming my family into Forest and Bird, a magazine with pictures of bush, sky, and stuff, a card listing all the activities in the Wellington area for three months (they were all walks, unfortunately), and then a personal letter to me saying that the Lodge booking had been made for two people for May 21, 22, and 23. I turned the envelope upside down and out fell a huge key!

Mom looked really interested then. She stopped reading the paper. "What's that?"

"Just a key."

"For what?"

"My vacation house."

"What?"

"I've organized my May vacation, like you suggested."

"What vacation house? Where?"

"Never you mind."

"Oh, I see. Well, do let me know what days you won't be here for meals."

She uncrossed and recrossed her legs, as she often did when she was acting more hoity-toity than she felt.

I stared at the key—the key to my future as an Auckland downtown lawyer, property developer, and heir to an inestimable fortune.

My dream was broken by Mom mussing up my hair again, rubbing my shoulder, and saying, "Come on, Henry, let's be knowing."

So I told her. Not everything, of course. Just that I, Henry Jollifer, solo child, was going to the Forest and Bird Lodge, Ruapehu, for three nights and four days of intensive volcano study, and that I could select a companion from among the throngs at school craving what sparse companionship I could offer them in my rare leisure moments.

And you know what she did? She burst out laughing.

"Henry, darl. You are so funny. And wonderful. I never thought you'd arrange anything for yourself."

I shrugged and kind of blushed. It was embarrassing.

"How could you afford it?" asked Mom, more threateningly, after she'd read the letter.

"I used my savings. That stuff Aunt Ellen gave me for Christmas, and the money Dad occasionally gives me when I'm over there. I've saved it all up."

She went really strange. I swear she wiped her eyes on the curtain (the table's right next to the window and she never has cloth napkins like Lesley's dad would have). She looked at me weirdly, her mouth all loose, then she kind of dived for me. I wasn't expecting it. I thought she'd be furious I'd taken my savings without asking her. But no, there I was, locked in a stifling embrace, my neck bent back at a dangerous angle and a dungaree button gouging a hole in my cheek.

When I was on the point of being asphyxiated by my anaconda mama, she released me. I guess Lesley will be able to fight his way out of these clinches without suffering as much crushing as I got. His rugby skills will be useful. I'm a bit worried for Lesley's dad though.

"Look, Mom, there's a folded-up poster of a baby penguin—"

"Henry! My darling. I do love you!"

This was terrible. She wasn't even listening to me.

"Henry, I just never realized how serious you were about that silly old school project of yours. Oh, Henry, would you consider me for a vacation companion?"

She was getting really bonkers. She even held my hand like I had to hold Rachel Brown's in a school play I'd been in once—just a play for our reading group, but that was enough. It put me off that Prince and Princess stuff for ever.

But I had to keep my resolution in sight here, as I knew I had Mom right where I wanted her.

"I'll consider it," I said gruffly, "if you make a lemon meringue pie for dessert."

"Done!" she shrieked.

And so it was arranged. I, Henry, had done my first successful wheeling and dealing. It's obvious my talents are completely wasted here in Wellington, New Zealand.

Dear Lesley,
Just a quick note.

I'm busy studying maps of Tongariro National Park, and catalogs from hiking shops and outdoorwear outfitters.

It is arranged. We are booked into the Forest and Bird Lodge on the 21st, 22nd, and 23rd of May. See you there!
Henry, son of Hairy Man

PS   Mom falls for men with beards and ponytails. Make sure your dad doesn't have a haircut before the trip.

18

That night I was trying to get to sleep when the phone rang. This is what I heard.

"Jill . . . so what's been happening with you, eh? . . . Uh ha . . . uh ha. Well, you're well rid of him. I told you what a sexist creep I thought he was, didn't I? . . . Hmmm . . . hmmm . . . hmmm . . . No. . . . Wow! Amazing. Heh, well, wait till I tell you what's been happening on the home front. . . . No, nothing like that! . . . No. Henry's organized a complete vacation for us in May and he's even got AA maps, Lands and Survey booklets, and Forest and Bird info, the lot. . . . Oh, at Ruapehu. . . . Yes, I know . . . I suspect he's up to something. . . . Hey, Jill, you've got older kids. He's—er—not old enough to be girl-crazy, is he? . . . No, you don't think so either, eh? . . . No, he's far too immature, but you just never know these days. Anyway, he's mad to go so we're off, yes, May twenty-first to twenty-third. Could you mark that in your diary, to feed Supercushion? Oh, Supercushion isn't himself at present. He's got an abscess, I think, and he's much slower and sleeps more than ever. Keep an eye on him, won't you? . . . Oh no, I'm not looking for men up there, Jill. I'm totally uninterested in men now. I've seen the light. Look, pop around after the union meeting. I'll put the gin in the freezer. See ya. Bye."

How can she call me immature? I'm twelve. Does she expect me to have wrinkled skin and a walking stick? I was so furious I set my flashlight up and wrote to Lesley. I knew he'd understand.

Dear Lesley,
Mom is a pain tonight. When she's on the phone to Jill she reminds me of the silly girls who sit in the front of our class. They're always giggling about something and if you ask them what, they say, "Nothing," and shriek with laughter. It's very sobering to realize my mom was once a girl like that.

Gavin's coming back to school on Monday. They've put him in another class. Boy, is he mad!
Cheers,
Henry

I didn't tell Lesley about being called immature. He sounded so physically advanced I had a suspicion he was probably a new-model human and I was the sort who would soon be obsolete.

Ten days to go. I was dying to get out of the rough, uncouth life I led down here and mix with the bankers and lawyers and powerful people in Auckland. Spanzini told me that maybe I could just start learning the business of the family firm right away and not have to go to high school at all.

Four days later I got a reply. That was really fast!

Dear Henry,
Dad and I have just had a boxing match during which I knocked him out. He's being attended to by our personal physician and I'm resting before I go on stage at the Town Hall tonight playing a violin concerto with the Symphony Orchestra. Thank goodness this is a quiet time in my life. When it gets really busy with the Olympic trials and my Mastermind appearances, I am absolutely frantic. But I wouldn't change it for the world. I love life. Do you?

I hope your mother won't be too giggly when she meets my dad. I don't think he'd think a lot of that sort of woman.

I'm sure he expects women to behave with dignity. The women in his office do. We know your mom's just what he needs to cheer him up—but not too suddenly.

Hey, I'm really excited about this venture. And Dad says I've worked hard this term and need a break, so I know that means he'll buy me something as a present, something big and special, because he goes in for special rewards.

Do you realize it's only sixteen days to go!!

Here is a list of what I'm taking:

one backpack
jeans
shorts for walking
T-shirt
bush shirt
down jacket
new hiking boots
new jogging suit for evenings
toiletries, including shaving gear
swimsuit
10 books
cameras—video and 35-mm
binoculars
notebook
diary
Walkman and heap of cassettes

What are you taking?

We must now organize how we will recognize each other.

I shall be wearing a new gray sweatshirt and pants, blue running shoes and—just in case anyone else wears the same— a long knitted scarf of red-and-blue stripes, my soccer scarf.

I am of medium height and build, have brown curly hair, and, now, am clean-shaven.

I enclose a Xerox copy of the booking I've made at the Lodge so it's proof of my commitment to this project.
OK. See you there!!!!!
Lesley

I wrote back immediately, because Lesley had made a terrible mistake.

19

Dear Lesley,
Horrors! THERE HAS BEEN A TERRIBLE MISTAKE!
   Your letter, with the Xerox enclosed, arrived today and,
oh brother, thank goodness it did because—I've booked for
the 21, 22, 23 May and you've booked for the 28, 29, 30!
   I've eaten a ton of crackers with jelly on them and still
there's a burning hole in my stomach. Must be tension.
   I await Mom's arrival home from work. I have to work on
her to delay the trip. I've already phoned Forest and Bird
and changed our booking to the same days as yours. I told
the person in the office it was a family reunion and we had
to be there the same days as you. He was very helpful.
   I'll have to have another cracker. Then I'll bike down to
the post office with this to catch the 4 p.m. mail.
Hurried Henry

PS   Don't worry. I regard it as a test of my managing di-
rector skills. I will sort the mess out.

I mailed the letter, rushed home, cleaned up the cracker
crumbs, and poured a cup of tea for Mom. She was due in
any minute.

Half an hour later she arrived, with plastic bags, paper
bags, and boxes. She'd been shopping.

"Oh, Henry, I'd love a cup of tea," she said.

"It's poured, Mom. I've got it all ready."

"That! That's from last night."

"No. Honest. I made it now for you."

"Ugh. It's stone cold and looks like a fried egg on top. Chuck it away. Oooh, my feet. That poor toe still isn't right."

"What did you buy?" I said, plugging the kettle in again.

"Stuff for our trip. Hope it fits you."

"Me! But I didn't choose it."

"Aw, it's lovely stuff, Henry, and it was on sale. Very cheap."

I looked through the packages while she slurped her new tea.

White shorts!

"I am not wearing those!"

"Of course you are."

"I never wear white shorts, only black ones."

"Tough."

A blue sweatshirt with pink writing on it saying "I'm with this geek" and a hand pointing. Yuck. Real tasteless.

White socks.

"White socks! I never wear white socks."

"That's all they had in the sale, dear."

Two pairs of new underwear. She's always buying me new underwear and I don't need it. I've got stockpiles of it in my drawers.

In the last bag was a weird heavy plastic thing that looked like a tent with a hood.

"What is that?"

"A poncho, darling. We're each having one, in case it rains on our hikes."

"But it's hideous. I can't wear that. I'd look like a marquis out for a walk."

"Don't be silly. They're what the experts wear. The man in the shop told me. It's cheaper than a raincoat and it covers your pack."

"What pack?"

"Oh, I'll have the pack. I've borrowed Jill's big one. You can have your schoolbag."

"My schoolbag!"

"Of course. It'll be perfect."

"But Mom, I'm not going to the mountain looking like a walking tent with a goody-goody schoolboy underneath it with white socks and a schoolbag on. I can't."

"Of course you can."

"I can't. I'm not going."

I stormed out of the room. It was the most awful moment of my entire life.

Even Spanzini was useless. I was in despair. My life is so full of humiliations. I guess I was as low as it's possible to go. But the light at the end of the tunnel gave me strength. I got out of bed, where I'd buried myself with the horrible teddy bears, and went back to confront Mom with the big problem. I can tell you I was not looking forward to it.

"Mom?"

"Yes, dear. Better now?"

I took a deep breath and counted to ten, then I blurted out, "I've made a mistake. We can't go on the day I marked on the calendar."

"What? I've spent all this money and—"

"I mean, it's the next week, the twenty-eighth, twenty-ninth, and thirtieth."

"You mean I needn't have rushed around town in my lunch hour and after work getting all this stuff today?"

"Can we still go on the twenty-eighth, twenty-ninth, and thirtieth?"

"I don't know. I'm too tired right now to work it out. The kettle's boiling over, can't you hear it? Pour me another cup and then disappear for half an hour."

I set the kitchen timer for half an hour and then I went and lay on the teddy bears with Supercushion and Spanzini. I've used this procedure of setting the timer before in times of great emergency. Mom feels better when she knows there's a definite time limit to her misery.

I wrote my last letter to Lesley.

Dear Lesley,
It's been a great strain telling Mom the trip is later than she'd thought, but I think it's all fixed up now.
I shall be wearing:
Sneakers
White socks and shorts (the very latest fashion in Welling-ton. Of course it mightn't have reached Auckland yet)
A blue sweatshirt
If raining, a mountaineer's poncho modeled on the ones Peruvian Indians have perfected after centuries of out-door living on mountains
I have brown hair, straight and the normal length, brown eyes, very flat feet, and an appendix scar. I am clean-shaven but have thick down on my legs and arms. This makes me really suited to mountain conditions.
Well, what more can I say? I hope our plan works. Have a good trip down. Looking forward to seeing you in the flesh,
Hopeful Henry

I biked off to the post office with the letter and while I was there called Dad from the phone booth. I just suddenly felt that he might understand about the clothes problem.

"Hi—er—Amanda. Is Dad there?"

There was a long pause before I heard, "Oh, yeah, is that you, Henry?"

"Sure is."

She went to get Dad. There was an even longer pause, then he came to the phone.

"Hello, Henry?"

"Dad. Could you help me? I have a problem with clothes for this vacation."

"Vacation?"

"Yes. Didn't we tell you? We're going to Ruapehu."

"Great. Who with?"

"Mom."

"Just Mom?"

"What d'you mean?"

"Well, any mates going along too?"

"No. But I've got one up there, a pen pal. We've arranged to meet."

"Great. That'll be good for you. Get you away from women for a bit. You need more friends. That's the ticket. What's he like?"

"He's got a beard."

"What!"

"Well, he's shaved it off."

"He's not—er—a friend of your mom's, is he?"

"No! He's a schoolkid, same as me."

"Sure he's not a woolly mammoth?"

"No, Dad. Anyway, Mom's gone and bought me these awful clothes for the trip. White socks and shorts and a yucky sweatshirt, and I wondered what you thought of your only son wearing that sort of gear. I mean—"

"Sounds OK to me, lad."

"No, but it's white, sort of babyish."

"Oh, I see. Suzy babying you, is she?"

"Well, no—"

"I bet she is. By Jeez, I wish I had more time to look after you myself."

"Well, maybe you could buy me some, you know, more grown-up gear?"

"Hmm. Well, I don't know. I give your mom an allowance for my share of your clothes."

84

"But, Dad, this new friend will think I'm a drip. He's in rugby and doing boxing and—"

"I see. You want to be one of the lads, eh? Well, you must be growing up, Henry. Look, get down to my garage tomorrow and I'll give you a check and you can buy what you like for the trip."

"Choice, Dad. See ya. Bye."

When I got home Mom was making shepherd's pie with beans instead of meat. It looked disgusting.

"Yuck!" I said.

"Shut up. This'll make you healthy for the mountain."

I turned away so I didn't have to look at the goo while I talked to her.

"Mom?"

"Yes, dear?"

"You've got the dates straight now, haven't you?"

"Yes, I have. And that's great because Jill can come too on those dates!"

"Jill?"

"Yeah, she's coming with us."

!!!!!!

Life is harder for me than for most people, I'm convinced.

That night I was forced into a most humiliating role. I had to sneak out when Mom and Supercushion were watching a soap on TV, and bike furiously around to Jill's. I had to bang on her door, get her out of the bath, and confront her with my problem.

I can hardly write about it. It was so embarrassing.

Jill thought I was having problems with Mom and was all cooey and kept saying, "It's your age, Henry." Then I said that I didn't want her to come on the trip with us. She looked really hurt, and then she sort of closed off.

"Did Suzy send you?" she asked.

"No. Heavens no. She mustn't know about it."

"Well, what's this all about?" She gathered her bathrobe around her and sat on the edge of the table in her hall, by the phone. She didn't ask me into the living room.

"I've arranged a little event for her and it's a secret and no one else can come or they'd spoil it."

"Henry, look straight at me. This has nothing to do with your dad, does it?" Jill's like Mom at times. She asks the craziest questions. I guess they both have a low IQ.

I stared right at the end of her nose. "No. Absolutely no. It's just a treat for Mom from me. And it's the kind of treat that no one else can share."

That sounded very tame. I looked at the floor.

Nothing happened. The floor stayed where it was and Jill didn't say a word. I quickly glanced up at her. She looked a bit less shut off and then she—she grabbed me and—hugged me!

I was terrified.

She mumbled something about how good I was, and then (this is the worst bit), she sort of rocked me backwards and forwards.

I biked home feeling inside as though I'd been flattened by a car crusher. But, yippee, I had gotten Jill to agree not to come. My wheeling and dealing skills were getting better and better.

20

At lunchtime next day I met my dad, who was much more interested in me than he usually is. He gave me fifty dollars to buy anything I liked! I was absolutely mute. He's never been that generous before. He told me to buy good straight-forward outdoor clothes from proper camping shops, not to waste my time in any fancy places called "Men's Outfitters."

I rushed off to the Scout Shop and bought a blue-and-black plaid jacket which looks really great. And I still had enough left over to buy some dark blue sweat pants. I figured I could hide the white socks under them quite well.

When I got home Mom was standing in the kitchen sur-rounded by plastic bags of beans, nuts, muesli bars, dried fruit, and toilet paper.

"Oh, there's another letter from your girlfriend, on the bench."

"He's not a girlfriend."

"Come off it, Henry. I can tell a girl's handwriting."

"It's not. I wouldn't have a girl pen pal. Gavin had one. He never bothered to reply."

"Huh. More fool Gavin."

I took Lesley's last letter into my bedroom.

Dear Henry,
We are off today!!
Dad's decided that we should have a couple of days in Rotorua first, at a huge hotel with spas and hot pools and satellite TV. He says we'll need a bit of our usual luxury before we rough it in the Lodge. He's checked the Lodge out

with contacts at work, and they say it's one of those places where you have lots of bunks to a room. You share your room with anyone else who happens to be there. We'll be getting there before you, so I'll try to reserve two bunks for you in the same room we're in.

Apparently you cook your own meals there, on a communal stove! Imagine! Our parents will be able to get to know each other while peeling onions and cutting up meat! I'm taking a candle so they can have candlelit meals while you and I play cards and computer games. I'm taking our mini computer with a few game disks.

I haven't forgotten that your mother likes men with beards. I'll remove Dad's shaving gear when we're past Rotorua. Otherwise he'll just buy new stuff. But I expect the Forest and Bird Lodge is far away from shops, so he'll be unshaven, and that may stimulate your mom's interest.

I must now confess to you, my closest friend, a terrible doubt that is in my mind. I think that I might be turning into a girl. I noticed that even my handwriting seems to be getting feminine. Do you think you are turning into a girl? Is it just part of growing up? I'm sick with worry about it. We must talk about it when we meet.

See you very soon now.

Lesley

"Henry!" Mom shouted through the wall.

"Yes, Mom!"

"Come and help me pack this food!"

"But there's a whole week to do that."

"You may be on vacation, but I'm working all week," she shouted back.

There is no time to think in this house. Ten minutes later I went into the kitchen. Supercushion was sitting in a cardboard box, yowling. He must be upset we're going away.

Mum was chatting to Jill, who'd just arrived. Mom was looking kind of upset. I thought I'd better slink off.

"Henry!"

"Yes, Mom?"

"I want you to get all your gear and put it in that cardboard box over there, and then—"

"Cardboard box! I'm not walking into the Forest and Bird Lodge with a cardboard box!"

"Whyever not?"

"I want a suitcase."

"You don't take a suitcase to a mountain hut. Don't be daft."

I foresaw another dose of terminal humiliation.

Mom didn't notice any distress. She was too busy talking to Jill, who was now standing by the bench cuddling Supercushion so she didn't have to look at Mom. I know that trick.

"But Jill, I can't understand it. You were so keen to come yesterday."

"I know, love. But I just can't get away right now. They need me to type that ruddy submission—"

"Well, I don't think we'll go, then. We can easily put it off till you've finished the submission."

"No, it'll take ages. Anyway, I don't really think I'm keen to be on a mountain in May."

"Oh? Isn't this a good time?"

"Well, it's a very good time for you, I'm sure: but what I mean is—"

"Just what *do* you mean?"

Jill put Supercushion down and looked at the boxes of food and clothes. "You need a break. Henry needs a break. He's a good lad, that one. Don't you put it off. Look at all the preparations you've both made."

We all stared at the boxes.

"Well, I'm disappointed," said Mom. She started to pour ghastly split peas into a plastic bag. A cloud of dust rose off them as she poured. How can they possibly be healthy? They give me hay fever.

"That's the trouble with women friends, so fickle!" she griped.

Jill was horrified for some reason. I could tell they were both getting unpleasant with each other so I leaped in.

"Mom, I'm not eating those dusty peas and mung beans and the vegetable pâté and muesli with no sugar and un-roasted unsalted peanuts. You've got to take some ordinary food, like the sort we used to eat."

"Why?"

"Because they have communal cooking up there. We might want to invite new friends to share with us—you know, be social."

"I have no intention of sharing food with people who don't appreciate good nutrition."

"But, Mom—"

She turned around and waved the bulging bag of peas at me. "I am sick to death of my whining, critical friends and family. Jill says it's the wrong time to go to a mountain. Henry tells me I'm eating the wrong foods. Why doesn't any-one ever try to do something nice for me!"

She stormed into the garden and started trimming the hedge. Only Mom would do something that crazy. I couldn't bring myself to look at Jill. I knew she really liked Mom and I'd put her in a difficult situation.

She went soon after. I saw her trying to put an arm around Mom. As Mom was still attacking the hedge with the shears this was a real act of self-sacrifice. She risked amputated fin-gers at the very least. Mom shrugged her off, and Jill shouted, from a safe distance, "I'll look after Supercushion for you."

"I'm asking Joe-across-the-road to." Mom said this very quietly.

Jill looked more cut up about this than anything. She turned and walked off down the road.

The week was longer than usual, but at last it was the day before we went. First thing that morning Mom went over to Joe-across-the-road's to ask him to watch our house and tell him he could have our newspapers and any free samples of shampoo or dried milk powder the mailman might leave. She stayed for an hour. She came bursting back in while I was spreading all Lesley's letters out around me on the floor and organizing them. This convinced Mom I had a girlfriend in Auckland. She teased me all day. I told her I thought girls were drippy, soppy, and wet, but she just said, "Go on with you."

We had fish and chips for dinner. I hoped this meant that the natural food enthusiasm was ending. Then I had to have a bath and shampoo, and at last the long day, the day I thought was never ever going to end, started to darken.

When Mom was kissing me good night she sat on my stuffed teddy bears and said, "What have you got cooking this trip? Tell me the truth now."

"Nothing, Mom."

"Just as I thought. You and Jill have concocted something between you."

"Nothing."

"Now, I'll tell you what I think, my boy. I think you've got a plan to meet this girlfriend of yours at Ruapehu. Eh?"

"No, Mom. Honest!"

"Hmm. Well, I don't want any nonsense, *and* I now realize why you were so keen to go—just your own selfish desires. It's about time you started thinking about other people, like me, for a change."

She tucked me in too tightly, banged the light off, and went out without another word.

Life is horrifyingly complicated.

I couldn't get to sleep. Then I remembered Mom's shoes. I had to change the boots and sneakers she'd packed for the two very old pairs of shoes with stiletto heels that I'd found

91

at the back of her closet, so she wouldn't appear too short for Mr. Lacey.

I crept into the hall where all our cardboard boxes and the pack and the sleeping bags now were. Very quickly I changed the pairs of shoes over. Phew! Thank goodness I didn't forget it.

I crept back to my bedroom and stuffed Mom's boots and sneakers down the end of my bed. She'd never find them there.

21

On the journey up the island to Ruapehu, the Mini was the oldest, smallest, and tattiest thing on the road. Big red sedans with impatient drivers at the wheel kept going up behind us and honking. I felt ashamed. I still had to sit in the back seat, so I had a better view of these frustrated fast drivers than Mom had.

I was pinned down by cardboard boxes. It was very uncomfortable. By the time we got near Levin, after two hours, my right hip had gone to sleep. Mom kept shouting instructions. I was supposed to be navigator.

"Follow the map, Henry, love. Somewhere around here there's a turnoff. We don't have to go through Palmerston North."

"What!" I could hardly hear in the back seat.

"The turnoff!"

"What turnoff?"

But of course we missed the turnoff, went through Palmerston North, and ended up, angry and lost, in a tiny place called Bunnythorpe.

"Look, I can't navigate from the back!" I blurted out as Mom came to a jerky stop on some gravel by a garage that was closed.

"Now, where the hell are we, Henry? I've never been here before."

"We are at the Bunnythorpe Post Office, Mom. See that building next to the garage? We're on the wrong road."

"Drat!" She turned the engine off and threw herself back

in her seat. The engine continued to run for a few moments. We both sat up and stared at the dashboard.

"Hey, that's strange," said Mom. "I turned it off and it went on running."

"Smells awful, Mom. Smells as though it's burning gas, oil and paint in a lethal cocktail."

"Damn! Is that garage open?"

"No."

We both got out and went into the small general store that was the only other real building on the street. A man was buying a frozen pizza and some French bread. He was tall and messy-looking, with a very nice smile.

"Strangers?" he asked as I leafed through the latest *Woman's Weekly*.

"We're lost," I said.

He put his pizza down and explained to me, not to Mom, exactly how to get back on Highway One. It was very complicated. We really were lost. I thought he was quite cool.

"There's no point asking directions when the car's broken down," Mom boomed from behind me. "Is there a garage around here? I'm overheating."

The guy smiled at her and asked what kind of car she had. When he heard it was a Mini he was kind of delighted, as though we'd given him a present.

The girl behind the counter said, "That'll make his day. He's the Mighty Mini Mechanic of the Manawatu!"

He laughed and asked, "Has it been pinging on hills?"

"Yes, I guess so. I thought that was the timing. God, I'm so hopeless with engines." My mother seemed unusually modest.

"No. You're not. There are no gauges to warn you in those cars."

"Well, what can I do?" Mom sounded more her old confident self.

"Nothing."

"Oh."

We all went outside. He looked under the Mini's hood and jabbed at a few things.

"Yep. Sure is overheating. Phew! What a stink! It's the trouble with Minis. Too small a radiator for the engine, you see. Totally dependent on the fan to force the air through."

Yuck, I thought, this is one of those very boring mechanics who give you a lecture. We'd never get to Mount Ruapehu. I shuffled up closer to the radiator.

"Don't touch! You'll burn yourself, lad!"

"Oh," said Mom, "this is Henry. Henry, this is John."

I don't know how they'd managed to introduce themselves without my hearing it, but they must have. Mom acts so fast sometimes. I would have to be really careful at the Lodge that I got her safely infatuated with Mr. Lacey before she saw any other guy there.

John said it was too hot to fix at the moment. Actually he said *she* was too hot, and Mom said it was a male Mini, called Casanova. That was the first time I'd ever heard it called that. He laughed at this and Mom giggled and it ended up that we all went back to his place.

He drove our Mini and Mom got in his.

"Get in, Henry. We've got to follow him."

I tried to explain to her about our health project at school, when we'd been told never to get into a stranger's car.

She bellowed, "Don't be such a nitwit!"

No wonder Mom never went to university. She obviously never learned a thing in elementary school.

After a nerve-racking drive to his little farm we had lunch—pizza and French bread and fruit and coffee. Mom didn't even protest at the junky food, *and* she had two gins, which I'm sure are not health food.

John fixed the car outside on the lawn after lunch. While he was doing it Mom told him the story of her life. I tried not to listen but he kept asking me to hold things, so I couldn't get away. It turned out he'd known Dad years ago. They'd done some mechanics courses together.

I managed a wander around the paddock. I decided it was a paddock and not a lawn because it had lots of weeds in it as well as grass. I could hear John explaining stuff to Mom that I knew she wasn't interested in, but she seemed to be pretending to be very interested. I guess she was desperate for the Mini to be fixed. I was too.

"I've taken the thermostat out," I heard him say. It seemed to me that this was the stupidest thing to do if the car was overheating. "See, look, Suzy, this device incorporated in the cooling system . . ." I looked up from examining the grass, and Mom was actually peering into the Mini's guts. I'd never seen her do that before. "The studs that retain it were rusted in. I've had to use a cold chisel to get it off." She didn't even seem to find this boring.

I sat on a gate a small distance away and listened to another speech about 1949 engine types. I was sure this wasn't Mom's area of interest, but she seemed fascinated. Don't tell me a new enthusiasm for car maintenance is brewing in her!

He put his tools away then, so he must have fixed it. It didn't look like proper fixing to me. He'd just yanked something out of it, probably some essential part.

"Let's leave it to cool completely," he said.

He showed us his farm, which was quite small and not very prosperous-looking. I didn't see one white-painted fence. He kept strange very woolly sheep and a few huge clean pigs.

Mom kept saying, "Well, we must go," and then launching into another story. John sat on the veranda in an old rocking chair and smiled and laughed at Mom's stories. Of course I'd heard them all dozens of times before. She could have shown more consideration for me and been quiet, or asked me to tell some stories. Then he went inside and made more coffee. I thought we'd never get to the Lodge. I decided this John was a real idiot.

When Mom finally was ready to go she thanked him so profusely I was embarrassed. He told her to pop in on the way back from the mountain, and she gave him our phone number in Wellington, which I thought was really overdoing it.

Mom said I could sit in the front seat from now on because John said it was safer. She was in a wonderful mood. John had repacked the back and made the boxes more secure so they didn't rattle so much. I was thinking that this idiot had ripped some vital part out of the engine, made us very late, and now he was insisting I sit up front. Was this guy an enemy?

"Hey, John, how come it's safer in the front?" I asked as casually as anything.

"I've explained to your mom. Belts are better restraints than the back of the front seat is. See—you'd just knock the front seat off its mounts if you crashed into that after a sudden stop. And look at those mounts—rusty as all hell! You'd knock that seat flying just by leaning on it. No, Henry, you're much safer in the front where your seat belt's anchored firmly."

I spread my feet out luxuriously under the dashboard. I felt great. Probably this John wasn't too awful after all. The test would be when the car started. Would it blow up? I wound up my window and noticed that he stepped back.

Mom yelled, "Thanks. Be seein' ya," and the car started. Maybe John was OK. We yelled goodbye. I picked up the map and skillfully navigated Mom back onto the main road. She didn't seem to notice my achievement.

"Who would have thought something like that would happen in a place like this?" she mused.

"Something like what? It's just an ordinary place, Mom."

"That's just it, sweetie. Such an ordinary place and that is no ordinary guy. Quite a find, that one."

I gulped. So near the mountain and yet so far! What if

Mom turned around and rushed into the arms of that pizza-eating mechanic? Or any garage pump attendant anywhere along the road? It was crucial to my plans that I got her safely and without emotional entanglements to the door of the Forest and Bird Lodge.

I crossed my fingers, checked that both our safety belts were fastened, and prayed that we wouldn't run out of gas between Bunnythorpe and Ruapehu.

We didn't. That man John must have topped up the tank.

22

Just as it was getting dark and I was sure we'd driven the whole way around Ruapehu, I saw a sign: CHATEAU TONGARIRO.

"That's it, Mom! It's just a bit past the Chateau, on the same road!"

"Oh, is it?" Mom asked. "And how do you know that?"

"I'm looking at the Tongariro National Park map, of course!"

She turned and looked at me, a huge grin on her face. "You know, Henry, you are a champ. I feel I can depend on you this holiday. I really am looking forward—"

"Mom!" I screamed as a huge flax bush loomed up in front of the Mini's hood. Looking forward was one thing Mom had not been doing, and we were nearly off the road and into the ecologically sensitive environment.

"You nearly crushed an alpine plant!" I yelled as Mom twisted the wheel and braked. We ended up on the gravel shoulder, sideways.

"I'm tired, Henry. Thank goodness we're nearly there. You'll have to stop your chattering, though. I just can't drive with you chatting all the time."

And then we were there, parked beside a big two-story wooden building. It had a notice outside saying **FOREST AND BIRD LODGE**. We sat in the Mini, a bit surprised that we'd made it. I felt it was sensitive of me to just sit like that, beside my mom. I knew she must be feeling exhausted and maybe a little overwhelmed.

"Well, come on then, zombie!" she suddenly shouted.

"What are you doing, just sitting there? Waiting for me to carry you in, eh?"

I got out with a cardboard box and the huge key I'd received in the mail, and crunched over the gravel to the door. "This is it," I said to Spanzini. "This is where life begins"; and with that I put down the box, turned the key in the lock, and opened the door into a lobby full of boots and raincoats.

I picked up the cardboard box and managed to open the next door by transferring the box onto the palm of my left hand. I then walked backwards into what turned out to be a large kitchen. People were washing dishes and cooking. I felt as if I'd just walked into someone's house. It was embarrassing. Several of the people looked up and said, "Hi." I put the box carefully on a huge bench that separated this kitchen area from a large room filled with tables and chairs.

"Hi," I said to a bearded man who was washing up. He had his sleeves rolled up and I could see a very expensive-looking watch on his wrist.

"I'm Henry Jollifer," I said in a really loud voice.

"I'm John McArthur," he said, in an even louder one. "Have you been here before?"

"No," I said, very disappointed that he wasn't Mr. Lacey.

He explained about the signing-in book, and told me where the bedrooms were. I looked around the kitchen and dining room at the other people, but there was no muscly, brown-haired boy with a five o'clock shadow. I left Mom to sign the visitors book and crossed the dining room to the stairs that went up to the second floor.

Up here a long corridor ran the length of the building, with bunk rooms, bathrooms, and laundry rooms all leading off it on one side. No one, not even an adult, was in this corridor.

I tried the bunk rooms. I popped in and out of each one looking for Lesley. I came skidding out of one to meet Mom panting up the stairs with a cardboard box of clothes. She marched along to the bunk room at the end of the corridor.

"C'mon," she called. "This one's nearest the mountain," and she barged in. Two people had all their stuff in there, spread on two bunks, one above the other, but the room was empty.

The walls were lined with bunks, like big shelves. Each bunk had a mattress but no bedding, and a reading light. There was a window that must look out at the mountain but it was dark now and you couldn't see anything. A nearby stream made a really loud noise, and that, and the clothes and sleeping bags of the other two people, made the room seem friendly.

"Maybe this is the right room," I murmured to Spanzini, who'd decided to stay with me through thick and thin this evening. "Just maybe we've hit the jackpot."

We ferried boxes from the car into our bunk room, then we went downstairs to cook our meal. Mom was still wearing her driving sandals, so I realized my priority was to persuade her into her high-heeled shoes. I had a feeling this would be difficult.

There were a few other people in the big room. Some were eating and two were playing a game of chess at the living room end, past the staircase.

"Henry! Have you peeled those damn potatoes yet?"

I was mortified. I was sure none of these quiet people said "damn," and what if one of them was Mr. Lacey and he heard that?

No one did look like Mr. Lacey, except John McArthur, and he couldn't be Mr. Lacey unless he was here under an alias. But if it was Mr. Lacey, then where was Lesley? I decided to check the signing-in book after I'd peeled the potatoes.

Every time anyone came or went from the Lodge I looked them over from my good lookout position in the kitchen. But there were no boys.

The signing-in book was hopeless, full of adult signatures

that were illegible. I couldn't even read Mom's name. It was just a scrawl.

Just then a man and a girl came in. They went upstairs and into our room, so my last hopes were dashed. We weren't sleeping in the same room as Lesley and Mr. Lacey, and it didn't even look as though they had come. It was going to be a pointless vacation of walks in the nasty fresh air. I felt terrible.

The man and the girl came back down and the girl curled up in a comfy chair and read. The man went into the kitchen and Mom immediately started in on him, introducing herself, gushing on about walks she'd always wanted to do in some place called the Great Outdoors, and raving on about "mucking in together." Bits of red goo dropped from the end of the spoon she was waving around. The man just stood there, his back pressed against the fridge. Then he mumbled something and bent down to open the oven door.

"Get your nose out of there and set the table!" Mom trumpeted at me as I was innocently decoding the signing-in book. I jumped, of course, but the man, who had no experience of Mom's style of conversation, jumped much more. He dropped this nifty potato rack thing he was lifting out of the oven. I rushed in to help—which I've learned is the fastest way to shut Mom up—and nearly fell over him. He was crouching on the floor staring at three hissing and crackling potatoes.

"There you are!" Mom roared as she stepped forward to hand me a fistful of cutlery. Then her face changed. "Yuck!" she screamed, showering me with sharp knives and forks like daggers. "I've stepped on something!" She slid across the floor, nearly doing the splits, and steadied herself by clawing at the neck of the poor man's sweater. She yanked her sandal off and held it up right near my face, as though it was my fault. Then she whirled around and scraped it along the edge of the benchtop. I was so humiliated I nearly turned inside out.

"What was *that?* Never know what you might find in a place like this. Could be prehistoric moa droppings, been here forever!" and she laughed and whammed the sandal down on the corner of the bench. Bits of squashed baked potato landed on the floor. One bit stuck like a snowflake in the man's hair. He got up.

"That was my baked potato, my dinner. I'd prefer it if you cleaned your—er—shoe outside. Thank you."

"Oh, I'm sorry. Dear me. Please share our dinner. Yes, share with us." And she waved the wooden spoon at a saucepan of brownish-pink boiling glop.

"No, thank you. We will manage."

The man stared straight at her when he said this. Their eyes seemed to be locked in mortal combat, then Mom giggled. Yes, giggled! She has no feeling for atmosphere at all.

"Ooh, there's a bit in your hair." And she—well, I shut my eyes, but I think she picked it out, like gorillas do. "There we are," she sang. "I am sorry I stepped on your dinner, but you've still got two potatoes left."

We all stared. Well, I opened my eyes into slits.

"Henry, pick those potatoes up for—er—what's your name?" and she waved her potato-masher sandal from the two hissing potatoes on the floor to the nameless man.

"I can't possibly eat those now!" he spluttered.

"Why not?" she exploded. "Waste not, want not! That's what I say!" She swooped down, grabbed the potatoes, shrieked, and threw them up into the air.

The man held on to the bench. He looked as though he was praying.

"Bloody hot. Sorry about that," said Mom. One potato had landed on the bench, near the man. The other had whizzed over the bench and landed with an "erf" sound in the dining room.

John McArthur looked up from the magazine he was reading. "Never cook them alive, lass!" he laughed. Mom laughed back. I looked up and saw the potato man's daughter snig-gering too. If it hadn't been for my need to meet the Laceys, I would have run screaming out of my mother's life that very moment.

Mom apologized, but still laughing, and asked the potato man again if he'd like to share our stew. He said no, he'd make rice. "But maybe you could clean up this bench for me."

And Mom did. I was amazed. The man boiled rice and chopped up a huge salad. Mom moved our glop to an ele-ment on the other stove. They didn't speak to each other after that, and guess who had to clean the sandal?

23

"Dinner's ready," Mom hissed at the door.

I was upstairs, lying on my bunk, having a mental break-down. Spanzini was trying to fix me up but I was a hopeless case. His extraterrestrial techniques were useless when it came to Mom. He admitted to me that moms didn't exist in his dimension, so he had no experience to call on. He did suggest that after I'd made my first million I should send her on a round-the-world trip in the Mini. I told him I'd made exactly five dollars this whole year. At that rate, he said, I'd be 200,000 years old by the time I was a millionaire.

"Henry! Hurry up! I'm not eating by myself down there."

It was weird that Mom had bothered to come up and get me, instead of yelling up the stairs. I got the feeling she needed me beside her in the dining room. We walked down together and then I saw why.

The potato man and his daughter were sitting at another table. They were just starting to eat. Mom led the way, making the widest possible curve around their table. The girl looked up from her steak and grinned at me. I didn't grin back. There was nothing to grin about. I was so embarrassed when we got to our table and I got a whiff of the horrible smell of the glop. Thank goodness they were sitting a long way away and couldn't see our food.

"I can't stand that man," Mom whispered to me across our table. "I think he's the one in our bunk room. I've got to share with him! He's one of those guys who boss women around."

"Shhhh!" I said. I didn't want to talk. I was too miserable. I certainly didn't want to be seen with a gossipy mother.

After I'd managed to swallow a couple of beans the girl came over to our table!

"Excuse me," she said. "I think you must be the two people sleeping in our bunk room?"

I swallowed a whole forkful of beans and Mom said, gushily, "Yes, yes, we are."

"I wondered if you'd mind moving to the room at the other end of the corridor, because I'm expecting other members of our party anytime soon."

"Oh," said Mom. "Oh, indeed." I saw her look this girl up and down. Mom never likes being told what to do by people who can do it politely. I don't know why, but I do know that when people are polite to Mom she's always rude back. A terminal embarrassment was coming up. I bent down to check my shoelace. "No, my dear. I cannot move. We always have that room when we come here. My early-morning yodeling sounds marvelous when done out that mountain-facing window there."

This was a complete lie, but I couldn't do anything about it. I didn't look at the girl at all. I heard her return to their table.

"You see what I mean, Henry. Gets his daughter to do his dirty work for him. Well, he's met his match in me. I will not be pushed around by some rude rich guy."

I did sneak a look at them then. How did Mom know if they were rich or not? The girl seemed to be having a whispered argument with the potato man. After a while he left the table and went up to the bunk room.

Mom then amazed me with her stupidity by asking me if the girl was my girlfriend.

"Of course not, Mom!"

She smiled and said, "Well, I'm sure it'll be nice for you both to do the dishes together. Nighty-night, Henry. I'm tired from driving. The longer I sit here the more I feel that I'm driving the table around the room.''

And she went up to the bunk room too.

Four boys arrived in a big noisy group while I was finishing our dishes. I stared at them all. Not one of them was wearing a red-and-blue-striped scarf. In fact, the only person wearing a red-and-blue scarf was that girl, who was now back in the corner, reading.

Then I realized what the problem was! What an idiot I had been! I was wearing the new clothes I'd bought with Dad's money and not the clothes I'd said I would be wearing in the letter. No doubt Lesley was in hiding until I identified myself.

I rushed upstairs and started going through our cardboard boxes looking for my things.

"Er—could you make less noise?'' the man asked from his bunk, which was on the bottom level, across from Mom's. "I am trying to do some work.'' He had his bedside light on and was sitting up in his spanking new sleeping bag, reading.

"Sorry,'' I said.

"And could you just move all those boxes along, please? Otherwise I might fall over them if I get up in the night.''

I didn't like this guy at all. I looked over at Mom, lying in her bag looking at a map of the park, and she wrinkled up her nose and shook her head, which meant that she didn't like him either.

I changed as quickly as possible and walked down the stairs. I knew this would be a difficult moment, requiring nerves of steel. To walk down the stairs wearing white shorts and white socks and not look a total drip was a hard task, but worth it as an investment in my future.

I carried a book I was going to read.

Some people sitting in the lounge area at the end of the dining room looked up. The four boys hardly glanced at me. They were tucking into spaghetti on toast. In fact, no one watched my descent with any interest—except the girl in the comfy chair in the corner. She stared at me really hard. It made me feel very uncomfortable indeed.

Her face looked as though it'd hit a wall, then it rearranged itself into an expression of amazement and, well, pleasure. If this is what my wearing white shorts does to the opposite sex then I am never ever wearing them again. I went beet red, of course. It was a hundred times worse than the school social.

Then, slowly, she let a blue envelope fall out of her book.

Good God, I thought. That's the same kind of envelope Lesley uses. What a coincidence. Then another letter pushed out of her book. I jumped. I held on to the banister. It was one of mine to Lesley!

"Where did you get that?" I was so shocked I forgot my embarrassment.

"From my brother," she said.

"Your—*brother?* You mean you've got a brother called Lesley?"

"Yes."

"Where is he?"

"Oh, he couldn't come."

"He never told me he had a sister."

"You must be Henry."

"Yes."

Now, I've always prided myself on being flexible. This sudden change didn't make me lose my cool. It just meant I had to adapt myself. OK, so Lesley had chickened out. Well, not everyone's as brave as I am. Maybe he couldn't face me, knowing he wouldn't be able to match my expectations of him. I could understand that. And it didn't change anything in the basic plan. The only crucial people in the plan were Mom and Mr. Lacey, and they were both upstairs right now. I had no time to lose. But before I could do anything I had to know whether this sister of Lesley's knew of the plan. If she didn't, it would be a bit awkward to explain. Surely Lesley would have briefed her thoroughly.

My palms were sweaty. I sat down and opened my book and tried to look as though I was interested in it. I was really trying to work out how to question her. It was a challenge that would require all my skills.

24

We didn't say anything for a while, just kept pretending to read our books. Then she said, "You write amazing letters."

"You mean he showed them to you?"

"Oh, yeah. No secrets between us."

"None at all?" I said this suggestively.

"None," she said.

I coughed. "Um—er—is that your dad with you?"

"Yes, indeed it is. He's cross at the moment because I hid his razor and he hasn't shaved since we've been here."

"Oh," I said. Then I risked a cunning question. "Why did you hide his razor?"

"Oh, no reason," she said, and tossed her curly hair about. "Is that your mom sleeping in the bunk across from my dad?"

"Yes."

"Oh."

"Do you think they like each other?" I asked very casually.

"No, I don't," she said.

"Oh."

"Your mom's great," she said.

"Not to live with," I said.

"She's, well, honest, isn't she? I mean, she's not polite in that unnecessary way most women I know are."

"She's not good socially, if that's what you mean," I muttered.

"Oh, come off it! You're like my dad. Too serious."

We went back to pretending to read, then she said, "Hey, can you play chess?"

"Yeah, a bit."

"Give you a game," she said. "I'll just go and get the computer."

We went upstairs and she went into the bunk room while I stood in the doorway, hidden in the darkness. I didn't want Mom making any girlfriend comments. Mr. Lacey glared at the girl and dropped the file he was reading onto his huge Antarctic-quality sleeping bag, which hissed angrily.

"What is it now? Can't you see I'm trying to work?"

"Sorry, Dad. Just getting the computer. Everything OK?"

"Huh. It's all right, rather like being at boarding school again. But that woman over there farts in her sleep. I've had to open the window."

I felt so humiliated I could have wept. That was Mom's bean and peanut stew.

The girl laughed. It didn't seem to worry her. As we came out of the bunk room she whispered to me, "Take no notice. He's often grumpy."

We were just going down the stairs when her father called, "Lesley!"

"Yes, Dad?"

"Don't stay up too late, please."

"No, Dad."

Somehow I managed to claw my way down the stairs. She was behind me but I didn't look around. I couldn't. I was in shock. Maybe I hadn't heard right. Maybe a brother and sister in the same family could have the same name.

Maybe.

She didn't look at me all the way across the room. I didn't say anything. She plugged the computer in and did something and a chessboard appeared on the screen. I knew I had to speak but I just couldn't. She sat there, staring at the pieces that were now lined up. Then I just said the first thing that came into my head.

"You were right," I agreed. "You were turning into a girl."

"Oh, yes. It did happen very suddenly." She said this very deadpan, and then we looked at each other and giggled, and then we started to laugh and we laughed till we were gasping.

After that she explained to me how she'd realized I'd just assumed she was a boy. So she made up all that superboy stuff and I'd fallen for it. She told me it served me right as I'd said such horrible things about girls. I told her that was because I didn't know many girls. She said I should get to know some. She even told me she'd underlined all the sexist bits in my letters and used them in a school project on equality. I felt done in. I asked her why she kept writing to me and she said she *loved* my letters. They cheered her up. I began to feel a bit better. We talked and giggled and played chess till 1 a.m. and then sneaked into our bunk room.

Mom and Lesley's dad were asleep, thank goodness. Mr. Lacey was snoring with an unpleasant gurgle at the end of each snore. It was nice to know he had his imperfections.

Our cardboard boxes had all been stored under Mom's bunk, so it took me ages to find my pajamas in the dark. I didn't want to change into them in front of Lesley. I planned to keep looking in the boxes until she was asleep, then I'd climb up to my bunk above Mom's, and change inside my sleeping bag. But Lesley solved the problem by taking her things to the bathroom along the corridor. I quickly realized I'd better be seen to be clean and sneaked down the corridor as well. Luckily there was a men's as well as a women's bathroom. I tested the shower, ran all the taps, and flushed the toilets. Then I changed and crept back to our bunk room.

Lesley was already in her sleeping bag. She had her light on and was brushing her hair. I climbed up the ladder to my bunk opposite hers, hoping she'd notice the stylish way I used only one hand on the ladder. When I was slithering into my thin kapok sleeping bag I found a note on my pillow. I turned on my reading light. Massive disappointment. It was from Mom.

Henry, honey,
I have worked it all out. She's a very nice girl. It's a shame nice girls have such turdy fathers. Why don't you get up early and make her and me a cup of tea in bed?
Love,
Mom

There, at dead of night in the Forest and Bird Lodge, with nothing for company but three slowly expanding and contracting sleeping bags, I felt that my mission was hopeless. It had been a great evening. I really liked Lesley. But why oh why couldn't Mom like Lesley's dad?

Then I remembered one task I had to do before I flaked. I climbed back down to the cold floor and ferreted around in the cardboard boxes until I found the knife I'd taken from the Lodge's kitchen after I'd peeled the potatoes that evening.

"What are you doing?" hissed Lesley.

"Nothing," I whispered back. I didn't want Lesley to know what I was going to do. It seemed to me that I was prepared to go to greater lengths to get our parents married than Lesley was, and I didn't want her to see the sort of methods I used. So I had to be sneaky. I cut the leather straps of Mom's sandals. Easy.

Mom had seemed to take a real dislike to Mr. Lacey, though. If only he had a ponytail. I thought of my father and his determination. He'd told me once about "tight patches" and how to get out of them. I resolved to make one final effort the next day. I got back into my nasty sleeping bag.

"What were you doing, Henry?"

"Nothing, Lesley. It's OK. Really."

"Good night, Henry."

"Night, Lesley. Hey, Les, shall we get up early tomorrow and make them cups of tea in bed?"

"Er, no. Dad hates tea, and he never has anything till after he's done his yoga and been for a jog. Then he has one small cup of coffee and one large cup of water, and some muesli."

"Oh."

"But we'll get up early if you like. You can see the mountain out that window there. It's choice."

"I have to make my mom a cup of tea."

"OK. We can do that too."

I lay back, pleased. It was reassuring to know that Lesley would make the tea with me. I felt really good about that.

25

Next morning all hell broke loose at about 6 a.m.

"Where's that damn razor? God, I feel scruffy. Lesley—I can't stand this stubble. Soon I'll look like a hobo. . . . Les, where are my nail clippers? Have you borrowed them? Les? Wake up! Don't waste the day just lying in bed!"

Mr. Lacey crashed around the bunk room getting his shower gear together. I prayed Mom wouldn't wake, I just knew this wasn't when he'd seem at his most attractive to her.

.As I peered over my bunk at Mom sleeping below, I worried that Mr. Lacey might see her in an unflattering light too. He'd put his reading lamp on in the predawn darkness to see the inside of his suitcase. Mom's hair was sticking up in all directions. I felt sure that Mr. Lacey was the kind of guy who wouldn't have a wife who woke up with uncombed hair.

He was busy selecting socks. "Get up, Lesley!" he whispered loudly.

Mom's green sleeping bag rolled over, two red eyes glared out of the top of it, and she yelled, "Shut up! It's the middle of the night!" Then she curled over again and farted.

I blushed so much I'm sure I glowed in the dark.

Mr. Lacey went off for his jog, and Lesley and I got up, got dressed, and went downstairs to make Mom a cup of tea.

We were the first up, so there was no one else in the kitchen. It was dark, and when I turned the light on, the switch made such a loud snapping noise that we both jumped. Lesley looked angry with me.

"Sorry," I said.

"For what?"

"For scaring you."

"You didn't scare me. No one scares me." She whirled around and knocked a saucepan lid on to the floor.

"Shhhh!" we both shouted at the lid. Then we both looked at each other and started giggling. It seemed really funny, shushing a saucepan lid.

Lesley solved this mood problem. She walked across the darkness of the dining room and flung open some curtains.

"We'll be able to see the dawn, Henry."

"Yeah. Can you see the mountain from here?"

"Over there, in the living room part. Out that big window."

We wrote our names in the condensation on the windowpanes. Lesley's taller than I am, and she wrote hers above mine. I watched her name dribble until it made little streams that flooded my name completely. I hoped it wasn't symbolic.

We went back into the kitchen and opened about twenty cupboard doors before I found a huge teapot, big enough for everybody in the Lodge. It had a handle on the side like a normal teapot does, and one on the top as well so two people could pour the tea.

The kettle boiled and Lesley agreed with me that we'd need at least four kettles to fill the teapot. That was a good moment—Lesley agreeing with one of my suggestions. The kitchen wasn't like an ordinary one—it had two stoves and four electric jugs. We quickly boiled up more water, and the kitchen cupboards started to drip with condensation.

"Where's your mom's tea bag?" Lesley asked after we'd emptied four jugs of boiling water into the giant pot.

"Here." I pulled it out of my pocket and floated it on top of the water. Lesley put the lid on and we peered at each other through the steam.

"I've never made tea before," said Lesley. "It's much easier to make Dad's coffee."

"Oh," I said, "Mom's tea's usually easy. I usually just put the tea bag in the cup and pour the water on top."

We both looked at the huge stainless steel teapot sitting on the bench between the kitchen and the dining room, between the light and the dark. And we got the giggles again.

"How are we going to get it up the stairs?" I gasped between giggles.

"I don't know," squeaked Lesley.

Just then the front door burst open and Mr. Lacey puffed in from his jog. "What are you two up to?" he bellowed, not at all worried about waking other people up.

Lesley stopped laughing immediately and said she was making my mom a wake-up cup of tea.

"Hmm," he mumbled, "it'll take more than a cup of tea," and he jogged up the stairs to have his shower.

That subdued us a bit, so we just leaned on the bench, looking at the reflections of our faces all distorted wide on the side of the teapot.

"Is your dad always that grumpy?" I finally asked.

"No, but he doesn't suffer fools gladly, he says."

I wondered what that meant. It seemed to me he didn't have much of a vacation mood. Could he be even bossier at work? I hadn't thought, when we were making our plans, that he might be a bossy stepfather, forcing me to get up early and go jogging!

"Hey, Lesley," I blurted out as she got a tray and put a cup and a jug on it. "Do you ever think parents are wrong—you know—do the wrong things?"

She put the tray carefully on the bench beside the huge teapot and didn't look at me. "Maybe they do, Henry. But so what? Dad's all I've got and I'm all he's got. I kind of feel responsible for him."

I stared into the teapot and fiddled with a dish towel. "Yeah. Mom and me are like that. You have to look after them, parents, don't you?"

"Yes."

We were both silent again, then Lesley said, "Come on. If we're going to look after your mom we'd better give her this tea."

We both lifted the teapot and poured some tea into Mom's cup. The tea looked like water.

"Right, let's go," said Lesley. "You carry the tray."

"No. You carry it. I'll need both hands to wake up Mom when we get there."

We walked slowly up the stairs.

"I hope your dad's still in the shower. I wouldn't like to disturb him."

"Oh, he'll be there still. He takes ages in the bathroom."

Lesley waited with the tray in her hands while I prodded Mom lots of times.

"Go away! Whatzermatter?"

"Mom, your tea."

A hand reached out from the sleeping bag and shakily groped around. "Whereizit?"

"You'll have to sit up, Mom. Lesley's holding it."

Mom wriggled around in the bag, then suddenly popped her head out with the most extraordinary grin on it. She looked completely loopy.

"Hello, Lesley, dear. Henry's told me so much about you. It's a pleasure to meet you," she gushed like a fire hydrant.

Lesley handed her the tea. "It may be a little weak, Mrs. Jollifer—"

"Weak!" Mom shrieked. "Never! It's perfect."

We both perched on the edge of her bunk. I couldn't look at Lesley.

"What shall we do today?" said Mom, with this dreadful grin still plastered across her face.

"Well," said Lesley, "Dad and I are going to do a day walk to Silica Springs."

118

I jumped in. "That's what we're planning to do, isn't it, Mom?"

Mom surprises me at times. She laughed and banged her hand down on her sleeping bag and shouted, "Absolutely! We have talked of nothing but that walk for days!"

"Dad'll be leaving quite soon. He's got everything ready."

"He's very organized, your dad," I said.

"Yes. Everything happens as planned when Dad organizes it."

I looked at her. I thought she'd said in her letters that she liked the idea of my mom's disorganization. Now she seemed to be changing her mind.

Mom shot me this embarrassing wink. "We're great organizers too, aren't we, Henry?"

"You bet, Mom."

Lesley jumped out of the way and watched, astonished, as Mom and I rushed around getting ready. Mom showered and got dressed in a bush shirt and jeans and big woolen socks. She flung plastic bags of nuts, raisins, muesli bars, and apples into the big pack. I threw the map in and stuffed our two horrible ponchos into my schoolbag when Lesley wasn't looking.

"There. Ready!" I said.

"Ready!" said Mom.

Just then Lesley's dad appeared in the doorway, dressed in shorts and a natural wool sweater.

"Are you leaving?" he asked Mom.

"No. We're going to Silica Springs and back."

"Oh, I see," he said. "Lesley, come down and have breakfast please."

They went, and Mom grinned at me. "Don't you worry, Henry. Your Mom won't let you down," she said.

Was she being cooperative at last? I was overcome. My knees went all weak and I collapsed on her bunk.

"Get up off my sleeping bag!" Mom roared. "We've got mountains to climb today! It's no place for lazy louts, this."

The injustice of it! No one except Mom would call me lazy. Think of all the effort I was making to achieve my NYRs! But as I've said before—I'm a survivor. I stood up.

26

Mom was rummaging around in a cardboard box, humming. The hum changed to a hiss and ended with a "Drat!" as she pulled out two pairs of stiletto heels. "Henry!"

"Yes, Mom?"

"Where are my boots?"

"I don't know, Mom!"

"Why are these shoes in here? I didn't put them in here."

"You must have."

"Don't be daft. You can't hike in high heels!"

"Oh. I didn't know."

"What do you mean—*you didn't know!*"

She advanced on me, waving the shoes above her head.

"I meant—nothing."

"What have you done with my boots, Henry?"

I thought that, although she'd never done it before, she might murder me.

"Sorry, Mom. I just wanted you to be taller," I blurted out. I'm hopeless under torture.

"Where are my boots?" she screamed.

"At home."

"At bleedin' home, are they? Well, my boy, then that's where'll we'll have to go, isn't it? Straight back, right now."

"No, Mom."

"Yes, m'boy. No more giggling with your girlfriend. We're going home." She was shouting, purple in the face, throwing all our things into boxes.

"But, Mom, I came for you!" I pleaded, my voice all high and whiny. "Lesley's not my girlfriend. It's her dad!"

"What!" Mom stopped punching her sleeping bag into its sack and stared at me. She seemed stunned and terrified at the same time. It must have been something I said.

"It's her dad. He's going to be your boyfriend. That's what we planned and—"

Mom sat on a bunk and threw two shoes across the room.

"Run that one past me again. I didn't get it first time around."

"Well, we, Lesley, who was a boy—"

"Pardon?"

"Oh, never mind. I'll start again. We planned that you'd marry Lesley's dad and we'd all live together. He's rich and has a yacht—"

"What do I want a yacht for? I hate boats. Make me sick!"

"And I'd be his heir and take over his business and—"

"Stop it, Henry. It's all too preposterous. Go away for a few minutes while I recover. I love you, kid, but you are crazy, just crazy."

She sank back on Lesley's father's sleeping bag and I slipped out of the room.

As I walked down the stairs I could hear Lesley and her father. They were sitting at the biggest dining room table and hissing at each other. I caught bits of their conversation while I pretended to make myself a drink.

". . . leave now. Can't stand that awful woman."

". . . OK when you get to know her."

"No. I need a shave . . . Chateau . . . stay there . . . more our style."

". . . probably is but this is so exciting."

". . . too many distractions . . . can't work."

I went over and sat beside them. I thought I'd make one last effort to achieve NYRs 1, 2, and 3.

"Don't mind me," I said.

"Well, actually we are having a private family discussion—"

122

"Oh, that's fine. I'm a very skilled negotiator."

Mr. Lacey looked furious, which wasn't what I'd expected.

I went on, "Some people get into fights with their children when they haven't got a partner to fight with. I know—I read it in the *Woman's Weekly*."

Lesley's dad looked as though he'd swallowed a spoon. I took advantage of the pause.

"You need a wife," I said.

I really thought that man was choking on a peanut from his muesli. I've read about this in the *Woman's Weekly* too. You go purple and swollen in the face and writhe around and are unable to speak. I decided not to turn him upside down and kick him between the shoulder blades to dislodge the peanut. No, I would be ruthless. I'd tell him the bald truth before I saved his life. I had him at my mercy.

"Yes," I announced. "You could marry my mom if you like. She's waiting for you right now, on your sleeping bag."

The peanut seemed to dislodge spontaneously.

"Lesley, get your things!" he yelled. "We're going to the Chateau right this minute!"

Tap. Tap. Tap. Above the noise of his chair scraping I could hear—what? I looked up. We all looked up. Mom was standing at the top of the stairs in her high-heeled shoes.

"Henry!" she fired, and stepped forward. She seemed to roll over on one ankle and then she was hurtling through the air. She landed in a huge pile of bush shirt, jeans, and stilettos at the foot of the stairs.

First of all we just stared, horrified. Then Mom made these weird sounds, like Supercushion choking on a fish bone. I rushed over and knelt beside her, my head close to her screwed-up face.

"Henry, you idiot!" she shrieked into my ear. "I can't walk in these shoes! I think I've broken my leg!"

I didn't know what to do. I looked up and saw that Mr.

Lacey was coming over. He felt Mom's leg very gently and said, "Indeed, I think you have." He went over to the phone. Other people had gathered, bleary-eyed, at the top of the stairs.

"Everything OK?" one of them asked.

"All under control," said Mr. Lacey, as he dialed a number.

"Don't worry, Henry." Lesley patted me on the shoulder. "Dad's a good organizer. He'll see she gets medical attention."

From being totally stunned, my mind suddenly went into hyperdrive. Medical attention . . . Hospitals! According to TV, hospitals are very romantic places. Maybe the situation wasn't as hopeless as it looked.

I crossed my fingers. "My mom's so brave," I said.

27

In the hospital Mr. Lacey spoke to the receptionist and the nurse, found a wheelchair for Mom, and pushed it. I wasn't even needed for this, which seemed strange to me. I was used to being needed in Mom's emergencies. I almost felt in the way, but of course I knew it was worth it—this adventure was bound to awaken Mom's sexual appetite. Come to think of it, I was hungry too. Neither Mom nor I had had breakfast.

I said, "I'm really hungry. Are you, Mom?"—just to get an indication of whether or not she was thinking tasty thoughts about Mr. Lacey yet. She moaned slightly, and Mr. Lacey turned around and said, "Here, take this. Both of you go and get something to eat. We'll be in X-ray, and then there's the setting and plastering. We'll be ages. See you both later." And he chucked me a crumpled ten-dollar bill! I was stunned. Ten dollars for being hungry!

Lesley and I walked back up the corridor. She asked the receptionist—I was still too stunned to do any organizing— where we could go to get something to eat, and very soon we were both sitting facing each other in this posh coffee shop. I had a strawberry milkshake. Lesley had an ice-cream soda.

Lesley stared past the hanging plants and out the window. I twirled the glass ashtray round and round with my middle finger. But not for long. Once the milkshake had covered my bare nerve ends I was back to normal—in control and taking the initiative.

"Do you think they've done it yet?" I asked.

"No, these things take ages."

"No they don't."

"How do you know?"

" 'Cause I've read about it. Basically it could happen as soon as they look at each other, if they're hungry enough."

"Huh? Bet they're not back from the X-ray session yet."

"X-ray! What are you talking about?"

"The broken leg. You asked me if they'd set it yet."

"I didn't."

"You did so."

"I didn't. So there."

She stared out the window again and I experimented with twirling the ashtray with my left middle finger instead of my right. The stupid ashtray whooshed across the table and landed in Lesley's lap.

"Sorry."

"That's dumb."

"I said sorry."

This wasn't going too well. But, persistent me, I asked again: "Lesley, do you think they've—you know—?"

"What?"

"Fallen in love yet?"

She was sucking the last of her ice-cream soda from the edge of the glass. She spluttered and looked up. "Henry, I'm pretty sure they're not going to fall in love. Ever, I mean."

"Oh. But how do you know?"

"I dunno. I guess I just sort of know."

"Oh well. That's that, then. The vacation's all wasted."

I handled that moment well. There I was, being told by this girl that my NYRs were finished, that my life of poverty and humiliation was to continue forever, and all I did was squeeze a leaf on one of the plants. Only a very perceptive person, like a bank manager, would have noticed it.

I recovered, and looked up at Lesley. Her face was all

angry—not what you'd expect from someone who's got a yacht and a computer.

"The vacation's *not* wasted!" she shouted. "Not for me, anyway. I now know my pen pal for real, and so do you."

"Yes, but—"

"You're treating me as though I'm just here to fit in with your scheme. What about *my* vacation? What about us being friends?"

"Yes, but it was Mom and your dad—"

"Oh, guinea-pig poo to that! Look, Henry, they're not right for each other. Don't ask me why. Forget that whole scene. It was a great scheme but let's bury it now. I'm sick of it. Let's do something fun for a change."

And so, well, we did. Lesley had this great idea that I pretend to break my leg and we go to the hospital and get a wheelchair. She would push me up and down the shiny corridors and I would pull gruesome faces and give terminal moans when we passed people.

It was choice. Superchoice. The best part was when we whizzed around this corner and I made my best most gruesome moan and there, right in front of me, was Mom in her wheelchair and Mr. Lacey standing behind her! She murmured, looking kind of frantic but powerless, "Henry, not you too!" and Mr. Lacey bellowed at us, "Get the hell out of here, you ratbags!" so fiercely that Mom jerked and went all white. We zoomed past them and out into the parking lot.

Lesley parked me under a tree and collapsed on a small planter box beside my chair. We were both breathless with laughter. I had plenty of time to look at her because she laughed more than I did. She was kind of nice-looking in a rather posh sort of way. I could imagine her becoming a glamorous secretary when she'd learned to put on makeup and stuff. She's the sort of girl who'd treat me like a corpse at a school social. I'd never get to dance with her sort. She'd choose a boy who could dance and talk at the same time.

"I bet you'll be a glamorous secretary when you're bigger," I said.

"Like hell! You'd make a better glamorous secretary than I would. Your eyelashes are longer than mine. What bloody cheek! I'm going to be an architect."

She sometimes made me feel I'd said the wrong thing. I never feel like that with Gavin. Maybe I should just stick with Gavin.

"What were you thinking of, Henry?"

"Oh, nothing. Well, my friend Gavin."

She started digging soil out of the planter and putting it in my lap. I threw it back at her.

"Gavin!" she said. "Hey! Henry!" She stopped throwing dirt at me. "I've got a choice idea. Why don't you give me, your pen pal, to Gavin? We'll still write, of course—I couldn't do without your mad letters in my dull life—but as well as that you could get Gavin to start writing to me and I'll pretend I'm a boy again. It'll be fun."

"Hmmm." I was torn between loyalty to Gavin and wanting a bit of fun.

"Look," she went on, "remember what he did to you with the jelly bomb? You've never gotten back at him for that."

"True."

"And our letters before had a special purpose. This would be just another special plan. You'll have to tell me what would impress Gavin the most, and—"

"And we'll have to plan how to tell him he's been had."

"Yes."

"You're right. OK. It's a deal."

I don't know why I agreed. I've got a nasty feeling it won't work out well for me. But I couldn't say no. I mean, she'd just as good as said that my letters were what made her life worth living. I was feeling kind of good. I agreed, and I can't go back on it now.

We stayed in the parking lot for ages, practicing three-

128

point turns and parallel parking. Then Lesley leaped up in front of me. "Hey! We'd better go inside and see if your mom's been sorted out yet."

I started to climb out of the wheelchair.

"Oh no you don't," she said. "You've got to do the moaning and groaning routine one more time."

And off we went. She must like me a lot—she pushed me all the way up the ramp to the fracture clinic.

Mr. Lacey was on the phone in the waiting room. I could hear him organizing something about hotel bookings. We sat and waited, and after he'd made four phone calls Mom was wheeled out of a room with porthole windows and swinging doors. She had a huge plaster cast on her leg, right up past her knee. The broken leg stuck straight out like a knight's lance. It was embarrassing. Everyone else I've seen with their leg in plaster had crutches and could swing along really fast.

She looked tired and worried. I gave her a quick kiss and she said, "Henry, I just don't know how we're going to—" and Mr. Lacey strode over, interrupting her. He told us he'd arranged for a flight home for Mom and me from Taupo for the next day when he said she'd be fit enough to travel. He reassured her that he'd drive us to the airport and she could lie on his amazing tilt-back passenger seat again. He'd also arranged for the Mini to be driven home by someone at the Lodge. I could see she was relieved, but I knew that was all it was. Relief, not love.

On the way back to the Lodge Mr. Lacey bought Mom a pair of sheepskin boots so she had some comfortable footwear. He bought himself a razor to shave all the stubble off. I guess that was when I finally gave up hope. He didn't buy Lesley or me anything at all, which I thought was a bit mean.

It was late afternoon when we all got back to the Lodge. Mom lay on the couch in the lounge, sipping wine. She was propped up with pillows so she could see Mount Ruapehu, and Lesley's binoculars were beside her in case she saw a bird. Mr. Lacey also sipped wine. He seemed more chirpy. He told Mom that he and Lesley would be spending the night at the Chateau and that if Mom would rather have the comfort there he would book rooms for her and me.

But Mom said no. "Thanks, Con. But I like the atmosphere here. And I've got Henry to look after me. I don't need anything else."

That was news to me. Was Mom now saying I was the only person she needed, forever? Would I become her next enthusiasm?

Mr. Lacey got up and put his jacket on. "C'mon, Lesley. Suzy needs a rest."

Lesley smiled at me and leaned over and grabbed Mom's hand. "Hope you'll be comfortable tonight, Mrs. Jollifer," she said. "We'll be over tomorrow to get you onto the plane."

I walked Lesley to the lobby. There was something I had to ask her. Now was the only possible time.

"Lesley, you seem to understand more about what makes adults tick than I do. Did you really ever, ever believe your dad and my mom would get married?"

"No," she said, just like that.

"Then why did you plan all this with me?"

"I wanted to meet your mom. She sounded like someone I'd like. And I wanted to meet you because your letters were so funny. I never meet people like you." She looked at the floor. It was an awkward moment. Then she suddenly changed gear, like Mom does. She tossed her hair back and laughed.

"Then I got more and more annoyed by all your silly comments about girls. I thought, right, I'll fix *you*, Henry Jollifer. I'll show you that girls can stand up to that sort of thing. I knew how set you were on the partner plan, so I thought that if I went along with that we'd meet and I'd be able to show you that girls aren't wet and drippy."

"I see." It was all a bit much for me to take in at once.

"Bye, Henry. I'll write."

"Bye, Les."

I watched her walk over to their car—the BMW I'd ridden in only twice, and would ride in only once more.

I watched them drive away. Lesley's automatic window slid down and she called out, "Write as soon as you get home, Henry!"

Ah, well, I thought, if Henry Jollifer is to become businessman of the decade it won't be thanks to Mr. Lacey. I'll just have to get there on my own. Or maybe Lesley and I could go into a business partnership.

"Henry! Hurry up. I want some tea."

"Coming, Mom."

Trust Mom to interrupt me then. She just can't understand the creative mind. I was standing in the lobby of the Forest and Bird Lodge, surrounded by smelly gumboots and muddy parkas, watching my chances disappear down the drive. And could she sympathize? Did she even realize the opportunity she'd missed? No.

"Hen-ry! Hurry up!"

I could tell her next enthusiasm was going to be her broken leg.

28

The trip home on the plane should have been choice, but Mom ruined it by embarrassing me. She asked the hostess if I could go up to the cockpit. Everyone heard her say I'd never flown before. I said, quietly but firmly, that I flew every vacation—to Disneyland. I tried to explain to the hostess, who never stopped grinning at me, that my mom's memory had been destroyed by shock when she broke her leg. But the hostess, who I think was subnormal, just laughed and asked if I'd like to hand the snacks around!

When we were screaming along the runway at Wellington airport the pilot braked suddenly—I think it was an emergency landing—and Mom yelled over the noise, "It's all right, Henry. Don't be scared."

I will never fly with her again. I'll always go first class.

Anyway, we landed. I had to push Mom in a wheelchair the airport provided. She was lying back trying to look stoical while I panted up a carpeted slope.

"Mom, how are you going to get home?" I puffed.

"Darling," she shouted out to the backs of the people in front, who all turned around, looking terrified. "Darling, I've organized a little surprise for you," and she lay back and chuckled.

We came to some swinging doors into the big hall where people meet arriving travelers, and boy, did I get a shock. There, grouped around the door, were Jill, Dad, Amanda, and Joe-across-the-road. We felt like VIPs as they all fell upon us with hugs and ooohs and aaahs. I was amazed Dad was there. He must have taken time off from a political meeting. He seemed real interested in me. Told me I'd have to go on vacation with Amanda and him in August. He asked me if I wanted to try skiing! I said only if it was in the South Island. I'd had enough of North Island mountains. Everyone laughed. Dad said he was delighted I was keeping my New Year's Resolution so well. Everyone asked what the resolution was, and well, what could I say? Then Dad produced the signed resolution from his pocket, the one I made at his place. I had to read it out—that bit about helping people in distress. Everyone laughed again.

Jill fussed over Mom and was really pleased to see us. No one grabbed the wheelchair from me, so I was the center of the group as we moved along.

"Stop!" yelled Mom as we passed the bookshop. "We can't come in," she yelled at the attendant. "Give us five Lotto tickets please."

Dad looked disapproving, but Jill seemed to know what was going on. "No. Ten!" she called, and she handed over a huge amount of money. "They're for Henry. There's two each, so you each owe me two dollars."

They all started looking in pockets and snapping purses and shouting about change, and I just stood there wondering what it was all about till Mom bellowed, "Henry! There you are! Ten chances to get rich quick. Thank you, dear, for the vacation."

I had to let go of the wheelchair to get all these tickets. Any one of them could make me a millionaire! Such a simple way of achieving NYR2. Why hadn't I thought of it before?

Then Mom turned around in the chair, and of course we were on a slight slope. They all charged off after her down the big hall to the baggage claim.

I stayed behind and called up Spanzini.

"Any especially lucky numbers, Spanzini?"

"I have analyzed every Lotto draw. I can guarantee you a winner if you use combinations of the following numbers."

Slowly and carefully I penciled over the special numbers.

When I joined Mom they were all shouting about parties and drinks. Everyone else in the baggage claim area was staring mournfully at cases going round and round on the conveyor belt, but no one in our crowd seemed at all bothered about my few but precious possessions. I could see that I'd have to take over and look out for our cardboard boxes. A small humiliation compared with what I'd been through.

Jill said she'd prepared a huge dinner for everyone back at our house, and we all drove off in a cavalcade. Dad's car was in front, with Amanda and Joe and me, and then Jill's car with Mom and the cardboard boxes. I got this strange feeling of how nice it is to be with people you know.

When we got home everyone stood around in the kitchen and Joe said to me, "Er, Henry, seen your bedroom yet?" which I thought was weird. I opened the door and looked in. Man, I nearly passed out! There, on the teddy bears, was the huge black Supercushion with six little pincushion kittens.

"Mom! Come quickly! Mom!" I bawled.

"I can't, for heaven's sake!" she yelled.

"Mom! Supercushion's had kittens!"

"He can't have." She dragged herself over to the doorway. "My God!" she whispered. "I can't believe it. And just look at that teddy bear quilt! It's ruined!"

Joe explained that Supercushion had produced the kittens on my bed the first night we were away.

"Well, we'll have to get rid of that quilt," Mom said. "Fancy Supercushion being a female."

"Just like Lesley," I said.

· · · · ·

That was two weeks ago now, because it's taken me two weeks to write all this. The kittens have their eyes open. I have a new red quilt.

Rachel's been pestering me to show her the kittens. I've said she can come and see them if she buys one for five dollars in cash, payable to me, not Mom.

Spanzini is in disgrace. In fact, I hope he's on his way back to his own dimension. None of his Lotto numbers worked out. I am in poverty again. Joe-across-the-road has asked me to do his lawns and hedges every Saturday. He says he's too busy resting to do it himself now, so I've started my first real job. And Joe says he won't deduct tax, so I'm bound to be rich soon.

That John guy from Bunnythorpe has visited Mom twice. We're going up to stay at his place next weekend. Mom can't drive at the moment and John's taken the Mini. He's spray-painting it gold! And he's putting in a new engine. I must make sure he replaces the thermostat.

I've been too busy writing this to write a letter to Lesley, and she's written three to me! But I've given Gavin her address and he's going to write tonight. He's bringing his letter around after school tomorrow so I can check it for mistakes before he sends it. I've decided I really will correct all the spelling mistakes for him. A joke's a joke, but even I couldn't be so mean as to leave in the spelling mistakes.

I'll make sure there's a letter to Lesley from me in the mail the same day. I wonder which one she'll open first?

Janice Marriott has worked in, and written for, radio and film in the United States and England. She now lives quietly in New Zealand.

Her favorite activities, other than writing, are walking and talking (preferably both at the same time), reading science books, and gardening.

Letters to Lesley is her first novel.

Are they really related?

The Sisters Impossible

by James David Landis

How can two sisters be so different? Saundra is a haughty teenage ballerina, and Lily is a friendly, lovable nine-year-old. They have absolutely nothing in common—until Lily starts ballet lessons. Bit by bit, Lily learns to like ballet *and* her sister. So when Lily finds out that Saundra is terrified that she won't be able to beat out the nasty Meredith Meredith for the one spot in the American Ballet Company, she's determined to help. It's time for "the sisters impossible" to make a deal…

"The story has wit, bite, and vitality to spare."   —*Kirkus*

"A top-notch example of 'sister power.'"
                                                —*Chicago Sun-Times*

A BULLSEYE BOOK PUBLISHED BY ALFRED A. KNOPF, INC.

You only live once... or do you?

The Lives of Christopher Chant

by Diana Wynne Jones

Christopher Chant would have nothing to do with magic if it were up to him—all he's interested in is sports. But when he miraculously comes back to life after a fatal sports-related accident, it becomes clear that he has no choice. To make matters even worse, he finds out that he has nine lives, which marks him as the next Chrestomanci—the all-powerful guardian of the world's magic. Quicker than he can say "Abracadabra," Christopher finds himself dragged away from all his friends for a crash course in sorcery—and not a second too soon! The current Chrestomanci has just been forced out of commission by a vicious gang of magic smugglers—and that leaves *you-know-who* in charge....

"This is a cracking good story!" —*Booklist* (starred review)

"Brilliant...a classic-to-be!" — *Washington Post*

A BULLSEYE BOOK PUBLISHED BY ALFRED A. KNOPF, INC.